Bob!
Some of the names have
been changed to protect
the innocent. Others
were left the same
because I figured they
are probably dead.
(Go Redskins.)

P.S. Don't let this
blow your mind!

MIND TRIPS UNLIMITED

ANTHOLOGY OF AWARD-WINNING SHORT STORIES

Scribes Valley Publishing Company
"Live to Imagine"
Knoxville Tennessee
www.scribesvalley.com

MIND TRIPS UNIMITED

Published by
Scribes Valley Publishing Company
6824 Drybrook Lane
Knoxville Tennessee 37921
www.scribesvalley.com

ISBN: 978-0-9742652-5-4

Acknowledgements:
"Whisper" from *Dancing Naked in a Haunted House* by Steven Curtis Lance, copyright 2006. All rights reserved. Used herein in "Haunted Houses" by permission.

Printed in the United States of America

TABLE OF CONTENTS

THIS ANTHOLOGY IS DEDICATED TO THOSE WHO KNOW THE VALUE OF MIND TRIPS

To the authors in this book:
Scribes Valley thanks you for your time, patience, trust, and talent.

WE HAVEN'T LOST A BODY YET!
A Foreword by the Editor
©2007 by David L. Repsher

Greetings and welcome to Mind Trips Unlimited. We're glad you found us. Don't let the well-used exterior fool you; we're open for business twenty-four hours a day, every day.

Are we ready to begin? Good. Please have a seat. Relax. Take a deep breath. Close your eyes...

Now, kiss your body goodbye.

Wait! Wait! It's okay. Sit back down. I know that sounded a bit...freaky, but it's all right. No need for alarm. You just won't need your body for a while. Don't worry; it'll be just fine in that chair. *We haven't lost a body yet!* That used to be our slogan, had it written in big Gothic letters over the door, but we had to take it down. It seemed to make people nervous. I don't get it.

Anyway, like I said, you won't need your body for a while. Bodies are restricted by the laws of physics and, frankly, just get in the way.

You are about to embark on fourteen different journeys which require your mind only. Lovely things, minds. No restrictions, no hindrances, no inhibitions. They can be as free as you will allow.

You can take all fourteen journeys, one at a time, in one sitting, or spread it out over several visits. It's totally up to you. While you're here, you're the boss.

Can I get you anything? Coffee? Tea? Juice? Crackers and jam? Cheese? Broiled elephant under glass? Fricasseed yak with gooseberry sauce?

What? Oh, forgive me. There goes my imagination again—off to

Whoknowswhere. The atmosphere here is very conducive to that sort of thing. Usually not a problem unless the boss is around.

Anyway, I'm just taking up your time here. Please, get comfortable and select your first journey. Take your time and we'll see you when you get back.

Good.

Uh, somebody want to come and wheel this body into the back room for safekeeping?

~FIRST PLACE~

THE WAIT, THE DATE, AND THE SINGLE GIRL'S FATE
©2007 by Kimberly Gemme

Saturday the 14th comes up out of nowhere and throws you for a loop. You think you've made it past Friday the 13th unscathed, so you're off your guard, all defenses are down, and then Saturday comes barreling in, the real kicker. I should know better, but of course I don't, in fact I choose Saturday the 14th to go on my blind date. My coworker Shauna has been absolutely dying to set me up with this guy who is supposedly just cookie-cutter perfect, very bring-home-to-meet-the-parents...meaning I'm obviously suspicious, because if he's so stellar, I don't know why she isn't gobbling him up for herself.

Possible solution: maybe Shauna's a lesbian. I mean, I wouldn't blame her, seeing as I'm about three bad dates away from believing that female companionship can trump anything a man has to offer. But I don't dare prod Shauna because she gets very defensive about her private life. Funny that she's the first to meddle in mine. Though who am I to be Ms. Picky Picky? As Kitty, the token spinster of my firm, not-so-gently reminds me, my breasts won't be perky forever, so I better snag a man fast. It doesn't matter that I can sport my Princeton University Class of '98 ring with pride and single-handedly support my very impressive Coach purse collection and mildly obsessive daily penchant for four-dollar Starbucks lattés on my (wildly) healthy paycheck as partner of my firm; no, all this goes out the window when you show up to the company Christmas party alone. How irritating.

I cannot believe I got to the restaurant before him. Really, I could kick myself. That's like a cardinal rule no-no. There's no way to look anything other than desperately needy when you're sitting at a candlelit table for two alone. The live violins and swanky mood lighting are mocking me as I sigh and glance down at my chipped French manicure. On my way in, I ran into the doorframe of *Arancio d'Oro Ristorante*, successfully damaging my freshly painted ring finger. As if it doesn't look lonely enough without a ring on it, now it's got the gimp nail, too. Too bad, because I have great fingers. My mom always wanted me to be a pianist. I'm the first to admit, I would look fantastic with a nice rock on my left finger, the perfect accessory to highlight any outfit. And yet, ugh. This nail needs immediate rectification, because as all we single woman know, men judge us by strict standards, and one of those is the condition of our fingernails. I know…but this is how I justify my bi-weekly trips to the salon for my forty-three dollar mani/pedi, not counting the fifteen percent tip— eighteen if I get Hae-Nah, the Korean girl who gives me hand massages with hot oil. She earns that extra three percent. God, those massages…

No, but really, I've got to focus. I've got a date to mentally prepare for. Who knows, this could be IT. I mean, this could actually be the proverbial Mr. Right. I bet he has a vacation getaway house in the Cape. No wait, maybe a cozy little cabin in Aspen. Ooh, that's better. A private, rustic condo in the Colorado mountains, and after we get this silly first date out of the way, we can jetty off for a long weekend of skiing and spooning. Actually, I can't ski, but I do make a killer hot cocoa. Thank God I bought those new fur-lined boots; I knew they were a good investment. Lucky, too, because I wouldn't have had sufficient time to go proper boot shopping on such short notice.

I look down at my hands to figure out which gloves I should bring when I notice the flawed fingernail again. Poo. That's right; I suppose I should get myself ready to win him over with my charm and flair for witty banter instead.

I'm rummaging in my Coach Soho Signature Suede Tote, Item #8A16 (it is fabulous, mind you) for a nail file when the waiter approaches the table. The ice cubes clink merrily against one another as he refills my lipstick-rimmed glass, and then he begins to talk. Lord, now I'm a charity basket, and the waiter feels obligated to make conversation with me because I'm only half of a couple, occupying what is clearly a couple-sized corner table.

"Waiting for another, madam?" He has nice hair, dark with a slight wave as it arches over his forehead, approachable face, and…yes, good teeth.

I'm distracted. Of course I'm waiting for another. Would I look this impeccable if I were here for myself, just aching to subject myself to pitying glances from around the room?

"Yes, actually, he should be here any moment," I reply, fumbling as I maneuver my Item # 8A16 under my chair and behind my coat.

The waiter bows slightly and says, "But of course."

He has nice hands, too: no calluses, and smooth, clean nails. Obviously not workman's hands, but I never liked workman's hands anyways. He's quite attractive, this waiter. I don't know what his name is, because this is a ritzy restaurant and the waiters here are above wearing tacky name-cards, but he strikes me as a Paulo. I think it fits him.

Paulo fills the water glass across from me, which is encouraging, because at least someone believes me when I say I'm expecting company. He has a crème-colored linen napkin tossed over his shoulder, accenting a crisp white shirt and black dress pants, complete with cummerbund. Very classy. I smile at him. He smiles back. Charming, too. Well, Paulo could probably never afford my habits, but at least I'd be guaranteed a table at one of the city's finest eateries whenever I wanted it. That's a plus; I could work with that.

I cross my legs, calling attention to the high slit in my otherwise highly professional burgundy pencil skirt. A drop of water sloshes over the edge of Paulo's pitcher. I'm all set to make a bona fide move on Paulo the Waiter when a man appears behind him, and Paulo about-faces towards the back of the room. I forlornly watch the "Employees Only" door swing shut before I turn to the intruder. Ah. Right, my date.

"You must be Jeannie. I am *so* sorry for keeping you! Normally I'm very punctual, but the valet situation was just atrocious. I really ought to complain!" he fusses, reaching for my hand. He brushes his lips against the back of my hand and my mood perks up again. I'll have to play the role of classy A-lister with this one.

"Don't let it concern you. I know how that can get. I'm just glad to meet you. Bard, yes?"

In response, he reaches into his wallet and produces a business card, which he promptly hands to me. Minus one for lack of originality in showing me his job status. I drop the card into my Item #8A16.

"What a lovely handbag. It matches your skirt to a tee! I'm always amazed at how women manage to accessorize with such acuity," Bard offers.

I raise an eyebrow. Almost alarmingly metrosexual, but nonetheless, plus 5,000 points for recognizing the über-fabulousness of my fetish.

"Thank you. Yes, it's from their new collection. I have to admit, I have a bit of a passion for clutches." I pet my purse lovingly. Bard smiles. Good, he has nice teeth. He has potential.

"Shall I order us some wine?" Bard reaches for the wine card.

"Please, perhaps a nice Chardonnay?" Not to be pushy, but I do prefer a good white wine. As Bard scrolls the list, I study my blind date. We women have to be on the defensive, because these thirty-something successful bachelor types *must* have some hidden deal-breaker fault that'll come up and bite you if you're not on your guard.

Bard's wearing a tweed sports jacket with a solid tie, safe, good; light brown hair and no recession apparent, also good; glasses that hint at intellectualism...I suppose we'll see. I'm not one to be easily fooled. Although, he does seem to be a regular Mr. Dictionary when he speaks, so maybe those glasses have some merit. I wonder if he calls them spectacles. I zero in on the tiny insignia stitched into his shirt and smile when I recognize the name as *Alessandro Davide*, the newest up-and-coming designer from Milan. Alessandro's got his foot in the door; he'll probably make a showing at next spring's Fashionistas Show. For now, he'll have to settle for being worn by Bard, who is now speaking to me, I realize.

"I had an exquisite Truchard Carneros the other week when I was here meeting with one of our clients. Perhaps you know of him, Richard DeLaurents?" Of course I know Richard DeLaurents: only the CEO of one of the most sought-after dot-com businesses in the city. I nod as Bard continues. "Richard and I dine together whenever the opportunity arises. A few weeks ago we were joined by Bill

Westerley on a whim!"

I purse my lips slightly. So Bard's one of *those*…a name-dropper. Unfortunate. "That sounds lovely. Truchard Carneros it is."

Bard leans back in his chair, the cuff on his sports jacket lifting up to reveal a gaudy, oversized Rolex watch. Why would you combine sleek Milan chic with kitschy accessories? Poor Bard's tip-toeing over from stud to dud on the date spectrum.

"So how are you acquainted with Shauna?" Bard turns his glance on me, his hazel eyes magnified slightly beyond what is proper behind his rimless glasses.

Oh goody, I get to talk about myself.

"We work in the same firm. Actually, we're the only two women in our department. It's quite exci—"

"Oh, that's stupendous!" Bard interjects.

I bristle at his interruption. That's bad enough, but if you're going to break in, at least refrain from using such archaic language. Stupendous? He sounds like my grandmother. My old, old grandmother.

"There's only one woman with the sufficient drive and manageability to be working at our company. Rhonda Billerman. Perhaps you know the name?" Bard asks.

"Yes, I remember reading a feature about her in the Up-and-Coming piece in *Business Wee*—"

"Oh, sure, that was a thrill for her, I'm certain! Quite an impressive honor for an otherwise unknown businesswoman." Bard's voice elbows in and cuts me off, again. I narrow my eyes. "I myself was featured in that magazine some, oh it must be six years back by now," Bard steam-rolls on. "It was quite a well-executed piece, from a technical standpoint, I mean. The author, Edwin Martino, do you know—"

Miffed, I reply, "No, I can't say I recognize the name."

Bard pauses, seemingly thrown off his track for a moment by my negative response. "Oh, well, never mind. Anyways, the piece focused primarily on the hush-hush project we were bent on releasing, and he did a splendid job dropping just enough hints to pique the interest of the readers without divulging too much of our highly confidential work. The work was mostly accredited to one Lon Wilson, of Wilson & Wilson Corporation, if you're at all familiar with…"

I stifle a yawn, and subsequently my eyes begin to water. Lord,

Bard is actually boring me to tears. Where is that wine?

Out of the corner of my weeping eye, I spot Paulo. I flag him down like I'm hailing a cab, but he maneuvers his way through the maze of tables with the grace of a figure skater. Ah, Paulo.

He asks, "May I offer you some wine this evening?"

Yes! God! Alcohol!

"Please," I say, cool and controlled. As Bard shuffles the wine card and orders our bottle, I blink out an S-O-S message to Paulo with my eyes. He doesn't pick up on it. Oh, fie on foreigners and the chasm between our cultures. Isn't the S-O-S code supposed to be universal? I sigh as Paulo figure-eights his way away from the table. Bard takes a visible breath and I can just imagine him plunging into another story, stealing away three minutes of my precious life never to be returned to me, so I hastily intercede.

"What do you suggest from the menu, Bard?"

He seems pleased to be useful. He flips open the bill with a flourish. "Well, such a delicate lady as yourself, I might recommend the lobster bisque. It's quite light and dainty, but the taste is just fan*tas*tic, nonetheless."

Delicate? Dainty? Oh, Bard.

"Well, I'm more of a steak-lover myself."

Bard's lips form a quintessential surprised O. "You are? Well, Jeannie, you are just a pistol! Steak! Then perhaps the filet mignon, always a favorite because it is such a tender cut of meat, just *superb* here at *Arancio d'Oro*. I should know, I've had it myself on many an occasion…"

I open my eyes wide and blink, trying to create the illusion of interest. I just cannot handle this talk of meat. "Tell me about yourself outside of work, Bard. Any interests, hobbies? Skiing, maybe?" I cross my fingers under the linen tablecloth. Please, something to salvage this man.

"Skiing? Oh no," he scoffs.

I physically deflate, and I realize I was actually holding my breath. "Oh. So you don't ski." No rustic getaway cabin. No cozy canoodling before a majestic fire.

"But I do enjoy fishing. Have you tried it, Jeannie? It's wondrously relaxing, a sort of primitive man-with-nature appeal when you're out on the river…"

I swallow a sigh as Bard starts in on yet another less-than-entertaining monologue.

"I'll just run and freshen up before our meal. Would you mind ordering for me?" I ask, not waiting for his response. I scoot my chair back and clutch my Item #8A16 as I head for the ladies' room. I slide by one of the restaurant's traveling violin players, who brandishes his bow with a dramatic flourish as I pass.

Bursting through the restroom door, I'm instantly pummeled by the overwhelming scent of schmaltzy perfume and overpriced potpourri. The mirrored wall beckons to me, so I oblige and peer at my own reflection. My dark hair still falls around my shoulders neatly, very news-anchor chic, simple so as not to detract attention from my fabulous creamy silk camisole. I open my purse and dust some shimmering bronzer across my chest; perhaps it's not too late to try to secure Paulo's attention before dessert. Reaching for Bard's abandoned business card, I take it by the corner and artfully pick my teeth with it. Well, at least it's good for something. I wonder how much longer I can hide in here before it's considered socially inappropriate.

I decide Bard can spare me a bit longer; I need some time to myself to recharge my sanity. I stare down at my legs, looking luscious thanks to my new GoldGoddess after-shower lotion. I can't believe I wasted a shave on this frog.

To my right, another face is next to mine in the mirror. I smile at the middle-aged woman who is coiffing her bottle-blonde hair.

"Lovely restaurant, isn't it?" she says, facing me.

"Oh, yes, it's just wonderful."

"I'm enjoying a quiet meal to myself tonight," she continues, kissing her lips together as she applies more lipstick with her left hand, which is ring-free.

Finished, she looks back at me and squeals, "Oh, I adore your handbag!" as she holds up her own. It's the Coach Signature Shoulder Tote, Item #2156. "We have similar tastes!" She drops her lipstick into her bag and yawns a little. "Lord, I'm getting too old to keep prowling the social scene for men! You know the feeling." She trills a laugh and turns to leave.

I laugh along half-heartedly. I suppose if I ever found myself simultaneously single and using age-defying hair dye, I'd have to laugh everything off, too.

The door swings open and a woman struts in, yapping into her cell phone and adjusting her shoulder straps. "Can you just imagine? Suzanne, that poor darling, twenty-nine and the only one there unmarried! Joan and Laurel even both brought their kids along because they couldn't find sitters! Suz came to my luncheon wearing this flashy, designer two-piece suit and she just looked so out of place! I can't fathom spending that kind of money on something that'll just go out of style soon, anyways. Well, I suppose if you've only yourself to support, you can afford to indulge in those silly things!"

I stand up a bit straighter. Maybe that Suzanne worked hard her whole life, always having to give twice as much to prove herself as more than just a pretty face with an opinion to voice. Maybe in college, she used to stay up to the wee hours of the night with textbooks, skipping lunch dates so she could get help from professors, then moving along the corporate ladder from secretary to assistant and exponentially on up, all the while maintaining an allure of professionalism. Why shouldn't she treat herself to some nice things? Who are others to judge her for her habits? Maybe she'll find a man when she *wants* to find a man. She shouldn't have to lower her standards, shouldn't settle for anything or anyone. There's nothing wrong with being a single woman in the business world who happens to love Coach purses!

If *that* woman happens to love Coach purses, I mean.

I hold my head high defiantly and push open the door to leave. I nearly collide with Paulo, who is balancing our decadent entrées on an oversized tray. Thank goodness for handsome waiters and food to distract me from the real man who's currently awaiting my return.

"Oh good, you're back. I was getting a bit worried. I know sometimes just the thought of such rich food can do you in," Bard says, winking at me in perfectly awful old-man fashion.

I stare at him, mildly horrified, and I want to say, "You take that back, Bard. Rewind to before you made this *stupendously* awkward." Instead, I turn to make sure Paulo didn't hear Bard's off-color comment.

Paulo slides my plate in front of me, revealing a miniature cut of meat with three asparagus stalks atop a silver dollar-sized puff of mashed potatoes. No wonder rich people are so slender. Oh well, I skipped the gym to go to the salon today, so I guess it's all relative.

"Thank you, Paulo," I say, tugging my top slightly to reveal my cleavage. Pausing, I remember Paulo isn't his real name. Whoops.

Luckily he just smiles and bows slightly. Leave it to Paulo to cover my social *faux pas* with elegance. Perfect ten, Paulo, perfect ten. He turns to leave and I resignedly shift my attention back to Bard.

"Bard, I...Bard?" He is staring catatonic at my breasts. I drop my head into my hands.

Picking up my knife and starting with the fork furthest outside (I think that's right), I decide to start eating instead. I eat all three asparaguses...asparagi...asparageese (Lord, I'm not cultured enough to dine here) in one determined bite and ponder my plan to salvage this train wreck. I suppose I can try the humor route. As we know, since I'm not attracted to him, naturally I'll be hilarious. It's the Law of Physics, dating style.

"So Bard, how can a successful businessman such as yourself find himself a bachelor in the city?" I raise one eyebrow to demonstrate interested confusion. Come on, Bard, do it for the team, just one good answer is all I'm asking.

"Well, I suppose it's because I have different priorities than other men. I'll tell you straight, Jeannie, I'm not looking to get married. Hell, I just want to get laid."

I choke on my potato puff. Attempting a career best recovery, I toss my head back and fake a laugh, making a *pssh* movement with my hand (the right one, not the one with the unspeakable flaw).

"Well, that's an interesting perspective, Bard."

He smiles smugly, and all I can focus on is the piece of pesto stuck in his teeth. I think I might dry-heave, and I can't decide if it's from the image at hand or left over from Bard's absurd comment. He is still staring at me suggestively, oozing primal desire, and meanwhile, the pesto is glaring at me. I stuff a bite of filet mignon into my mouth and run through a mental to-do list. Delete Bard's phone number from my phone. Check on the back order status of my Coach Detailed Saddle Clutch, Item #248F. De-friend Shauna. Etcetera.

"And how are things?" Paulo's voice brings me back.

"Delicious. Could we have the check?"

Paulo nods, surprised.

Bard's face mirrors Paulo's disbelief. "No dessert, Jeannie? Or just in a rush to get out of this place to somewhere more private? I know the feeling."

No, Bard, trust me, you do *not* know this feeling. "Actually, I've got an early meeting tomorrow at the firm. I need a full night's rest in order to function at my peak performance level." Bard seems to have sucked away all my creative energy and it's the best I can muster.

"Peak performance," Bard muses, his voice dripping with sexual innuendo.

I don't bother to hide the mortified look surging across my face.

Paulo returns with the check, concealed tactfully in a leather-bound case.

"Of course, it's on me," Bard says, reaching for the bill.

Obviously it is, you putz. As if I would pay for this social persecution. As he opens his wallet, a condom falls out onto the table, its cheap metallic blue wrapper standing out starkly against the tablecloth.

I want to shriek, "TYPICAL!" But of course I don't. I am dignified, after all. Paulo returns, sees the Trojan, and exchanges a man's knowing glance with Bard. I duck my head sadly. Too bad, Paulo, it could have been beautiful between us.

As I usher Bard out of the restaurant, I feel a hand on my shoulder. I turn and, to my excitement, a man eerily reminiscent of Pierce Brosnan is facing me, holding my Item #8A16. I shove Bard through the revolving glass door in front of me with a surprising burst of strength.

"Pardon me, I think you forgot your purse? I saw you leaving and I couldn't help but notice…" Mr. 007 trails off. He's on his way out, too. I stare at his other hand, already snug in a black fleece Northface glove.

I smile flirtatiously with a toss of my hair. "Thank you *so* much," I gush. "Oh, do you ski? I'm an avid skier myself…"

About the author:

Kimberly Gemme is an aspiring author and a sophomore undergraduate at Brown University, concentrating in Literary Arts. At Brown, she sings in a cappella and choral ensembles, and as a soloist in opera productions. She loves travel and learning languages; right now, she is focusing on German and Mandarin Chinese, and is always eager for more exposure to world cultures. Kimberly currently lives in Pinehurst, NC and spends her free time at home on the golf course.

~~SECOND PLACE~~

THE BOY WHO WALKED ON WATER
©2007 by Dan Sullivan

Aunt Bunch knew Buddy was special at five: he could recite every book of the Bible from Genesis to Revelation. At the time, she just figured the boy had set his mind on higher things since he was asthmatic and couldn't play rough outside. But, two years later the miracle at Leonardtown's *Auto World* left no doubt that the child was anointed. Aunt Bunch had narrowed her choices down to two pickups.

Buddy tugged on her sleeve and whispered, "Aunt Bunch, the Lord just gave me the word for you to buy the Ford. It'll last longer and gives better gas mileage."

She did, and within six months, the Dodge Ram, her other consideration, dropped a transmission on Three Notch Road just south of the Naval Air Station.

Later that same year, Aunt Bunch's older sister, Hatie, joked, "Mr. Arthur Ritis is payin' me a visit today, Bunch. He's bein' real nasty." Uninvited, Buddy laid hands on Hatie's arm, intoned something unintelligible, and, as she described it, "a hot warmth like a heating pad shot straight through my arm. Praise the Lord, Bunch! Buddy healed me."

After a few more healings like Hatie's, word began to spread throughout Southern Maryland. At eight, Buddy was teaching Adult

Sunday School at Glad Tidings Bible Church in Drum Point. Buddy would stride across the front of the classroom extending a Bible high above his head as he delivered his lesson in an emphatic falsetto. He would punctuate his teaching with sharp intakes of breath in imitation of the radio preachers he listened to daily. Before long, he had his own radio show every Saturday morning on WST, just north of Lusby on Route 4: *Holy Hour with Little Reverend Buddy Allbritton*. Technically, the show was not an hour. It ran for fifteen minutes, but in that time, the child evangelist gave Scripture-based advice to desperate callers on his hotline.

And so it would go something like this each week, as the boy preacher sat in the control room of WST, his head barely visible above the console, huge headphones framing his pale oval face. Regardless of the caller's age, Buddy addressed each one as "sister" or "brother":

"Well, sister, if your husband's looking at those kind of pictures on the Internet, tell him it's better to gouge his left eye out and enter the Kingdom of Heaven with one eye than to enter the Kingdom of Darkness with good eyesight...."

And...

"Reverend Buddy, last night, just about eight o'clock, Jesus walked straight through my front door, came right into my kitchen and operated on me: Jesus performed open-heart surgery and gave me a new heart."

"Praise Gawd, sister!"

And...

"Reverend Buddy, the people at Catholic Charities are giving job training, but my husband told me not to go. I could sure use a better job, but...what should I do?"

In the background, Aunt Bunch warned, "Consider the source, Reverend Buddy. Consider the source."

"All the good deeds in the world will not save you, sister. Doctrine will not save you. Religion and big churches will not save you. In fact, they may just lead you to Perdition. Sister, it's the word of Gawd that saves you. And wives must be subject to their husbands, so sayeth Paul...."

And finally…

"Now, brother, if your right hand seems to be the source of the problem, cut it off. It's better…"

At the end of the show each week, the boy preacher would remind the faithful that there was so much need "out there," and that the Reverend Buddy Allbritton Outreach Ministry was ready to help "lots of desperate folks." Aunt Bunch reminded the faithful that they could support Buddy's outreach with donations by check, money order, or major credit card. Then Buddy would end each show with, "Well, folks, remember to live so the preacher won't have to lie at your funeral. So long and God bless." Aunt Bunch would then sing *Peace in the Garden*, and WST would resume its fishing and boating reports for the Chesapeake Bay.

While all this was going on, U-Dean, Aunt Bunch's no-count youngest boy was getting kicked out of the United States Navy. The psychologist's report said that U-Dean "Jimmy" Allbritton had "a borderline personality," "rage issues," and a "serious drinking problem." After he sent to the emergency room a Puerto Rican busboy whose whistling had gotten on U-Dean's "last nerve," he served jail time before receiving a discharge under "other than honorable conditions."

As soon as he got home, U-Dean bought, in this order: four cases of Miller Lite, a rusty 1997 Dodge Ram pickup with a rebuilt transmission, and two decals that he displayed on the rear window of his cab: "Twelve Reasons Why Beer is Better Than Jesus," and a confederate flag with the slogan, "Fighting Terrorism for the Last Two Hundred Years." He would have displayed Darwin's walking fish, too, just to get his mother's goat, but he was running out of space and money.

Now gathered at the dinner table each night, U-Dean devoted his attention exclusively on his little cousin. "The boy who walks on water…my, my, my…got his own little radio show each week…my, my, my. Don't you be looking at me that way, boy. The pride of Calvert County. You look at me when I'm talking to you, boy…"

Buddy's wide, watery gray eyes would fix on U-Dean's eyebrows so he could be looking and not looking at the same time at his imposing older cousin.

Aunt Bunch was tempted to intervene, but she was convinced the Lord was calling her to a higher path since He always seemed to be putting in her mind the verses, "Blessed are the peacemakers" and "I will keep my mouth with a bridle, while the wicked is before me." As a result, she felt led to disregard the menace in U-Dean's eyes, ignore his fists planted on the dinner table, and ask him kindly to pass the salt as a way to change the subject.

One night, U-Dean came home in unusually elevated spirits. O'Malley, U-Dean's supervisor at Home Depot, had finally caved in. The small, wiry man in the orange apron had carefully avoided eye contact with U-Dean and signed the form permitting the State of Maryland to compensate Allbritton while he recovered from his on-the-job neck injury. As U-Dean had repeatedly argued, with increasing warmth, you can't prove one way or the other about neck injuries. Plus, he had "a paid doctor's signed statement" to prove how bad he was hurting. The recovery would be long and arduous but offset somewhat by the bi-weekly checks from the State and the improvement to his mind by a steady diet of HBO and Showtime programming.

"Mama, it's about time that little weasel signed the paperwork. He knew if he didn't, though, I'd break his skinny little neck. But I have to tell you about what I saw at work today. I had to laugh my butt off. This young fool, about sixteen, was standing with some lady in the check-out line. He's standing there with this goofy look in his eyes, and, out of the clear blue, the fool starts barking. *Starts barking!* Then everyone looks over at him and the lady tries to shush him, but then he starts out cussing so you could hear him all over the store. I tell you, I laughed my butt off."

Buddy, looking and not looking at U-Dean's eyebrows, concluded, "Demon-possessed."

"What?"

"He's demon-possessed."

U-Dean tilted his head. At first, he wanted to tear into his little cousin, but the sudden thought of Buddy struggling against the forces of darkness and the scary-looking teenager was intriguing.

"Maybe, you could say some prayers over him and cure him or

something." U-Dean regarded Buddy with baleful eyes and a mirthless smile.

Buddy, looking and not looking, replied, "I've never delivered anybody before."

"Buddy," Aunt Bunch offered, "this could be your chance…to win more souls for the Lord, of course."

"I don't know, Aunt Bunch. I've never delivered anybody before."

"Mama, maybe Buddy just can't handle it."

Bunch concluded, "We'll just have to lift this up to the Lord."

Buddy was looking yet not looking while he thought about it and chewed his meatloaf.

***

During the next week, Aunt Bunch used every available means of persuasion to convince Buddy to cast out the demon that was in possession of the teenager. Sweet talk, veiled threats, tears, and fried chicken and cornbread had failed to tip the scales. She then appealed to authority.

"Now, Buddy, remember when the Lord beckoned Peter and called him out of the boat to walk on the waves? Peter did just fine until he looked down and trusted to his own powers. That's when he fell. It is not by our power, son, but…"

"But, Aunt Bunch, I've never delivered anybody before. I think my ministry is healing and preaching, not delivering. It takes a special gift."

"Trust not in your own power, Buddy."

Finally, the Reverend Buddy buckled under his guardian aunt's persistence and agreed to pray over the troubled boy. Tracking him down wasn't difficult. Clint McCarty, "the boy who barked and cussed in public," had earned quite a reputation in Calvert County. Many people there knew him and knew exactly where in Dunkirk he lived with his widowed step-mother, Myrtle.

When Bunch first appeared at Myrtle's door, it was abruptly shut in her face. By the third visit, Bunch had gained access to the hallway. The fourth visit found Myrtle expressing her frustration over doctors and diets and psychologists. On the fifth visit, Myrtle finally relented as Bunch gently reassured her of the power of the Reverend Buddy's preaching and healing, failing only to mention that the Reverend Buddy Allbritton was eight years old. The desperate woman agreed to Bunch's offer to have Buddy minister to her stepson, believing the affair would be low-key at Glad Tidings, whenever Pastor Armel Armbruster was willing to schedule it.

Soon, the date was set. WST decided against airing the service, but the station would send a sound crew to record the event, just in case parts might be useful for a special or to spice up Reverend Buddy's weekly show whose ratings were beginning to flag.

When U-Dean learned that Ms. McCarty had agreed to the deliverance, he rubbed his hands in nervous glee. To his way of thinking, life couldn't get much better than this: rolling out of bed each morning at about ten a.m., cracking his first cold one at about eleven, cashing disability checks from the State of Maryland while elevating his mind each day with programming from Court TV, HBO, and CINEMAX.

Then after supper, it was time to head on out to *Side Pocket Billiards and Bar.* Now if he could just find a way to get access to the Playboy channel without his mother or that pipsqueak cousin of his knowing....

But what did his heart the most good was to know that soon the boy who walked on water would be exposed for the phony little jerk he really was. When he thought of his small cousin—a midget in a suit and necktie—struggling mightily, yet unsuccessfully to cast the devil out of that young fool in front of God and just about everybody in Calvert County, a less than amiable smile disturbed the left side of U-Dean's mouth. Yes, life was indeed sweet.

***

The entire flock of Glad Tidings crowded into the sanctuary that rainy Sunday morning when the Reverend Buddy, Aunt Bunch, and U-Dean arrived from Lusby. Reverend Buddy was wearing a navy blue suit, a white dress shirt and red tie, and black and white sneakers, the only shoes that still fit him. He bounced around the edge of the sanctuary, smiling at no one in particular, cracking his knuckles, pushing down his wheat-colored cowlick.

A tall redhead, a hairdresser from White Sands, standing next to U-Dean said in a cloudy aside, "The preacher don't look like he could scare away a mouse much less the devil."

U-Dean chortled in agreement.

The atmosphere in the assembly was almost electric that morning for the many who had come to witness the deliverance of Clint McCarty. Pastor Armel Armbruster, however, had one huge rhetorical problem on his hands: how to present the ethos of the gracious minister and host to Buddy and his guardian aunt while conveying skepticism—but not too much skepticism—about the service itself and the diminutive healer, since the people who packed his church that day just might view that as disapproval—disapproval of something that they themselves were behind one hundred percent. Gracious and skeptical—yet not too skeptical—yet a firm believer; it would be tough to pull off.

What seemed to be called for was Pastor Armbruster's "suffering servant" ethos—conveyed with a wan smile and downcast eyes and a sudden brightening when addressed. In reality, sitting in the sanctuary with his arms folded and downcast eyes, he came across as a pouting, middle-aged man.

Aunt Bunch had selected the deliverance of the demoniac from Gedara in Mark as the foundation for Buddy's teaching that morning. When he was finished, Buddy asked all to rise and for Clint and his stepmother to enter the sanctuary. Buddy then asked all to stand and extend their hands toward Clint and Myrtle McCarty.

The entire congregation held hands and whispered prayers that began to rise and fall like the rush of waves at low tide as the tall teenager took the seat in the center of the sanctuary. His black hair was slicked back and covered the collar of his white shirt. His eyes were black and defiant. A trace of a mustache and goatee framed his full lips. Clint McCarty, the teenager who barked and cussed in public, sat tall and square-shouldered in the metal folding chair.

As the congregation continued its whispered prayers, Buddy came and laid hands on the boy's forearm. The Reverend Buddy started the deliverance by thanking the Lord for Clint, for the assembly of saints at Glad Tidings, and for the church itself, an A-frame building on a dirt road off Route 4. There were others to be acknowledged.

"We just thank you, Lord, for WST Radio for helping us spread the word each week. We just thank you for the Reverend Armel Armbruster and his flock here at Glad Tidings. We just thank you, Lord, for this opportunity to free our brother Clint from the grip of the enemy. We want to thank you, Lord…"

The redhead, in another aside to U-Dean, asked, "How much longer is he going to keep thanking the Lord? I think he's stalling."

U-Dean chuckled as he surveyed his little cousin's wheat-colored cowlick, his navy blue suit, his tie, and his black and white sneakers.

Buddy was about to thank the Lord for the generous free will offerings that the saints would in all likelihood be making for Clint's deliverance, when Clint put a stop to it then and there. The teenager shot up from his chair and let out a string of filthy words right in the middle of the sanctuary. Bunch lumbered over and covered the Reverend Buddy's ears, and above the rising falsetto commanding the devil to leave Clint, Myrtle looked at Clint and found her own voice.

"Just *stop* it, you all! *Stop* it! Jesus would never shame a soul like this. He'd never make a fool out of this boy like we're doing here."

For the moment, Clint seemed as vacant and lifeless as a shadow, but then he clenched his fists and let loose with another string of just the filthiest words any soul ever heard in two lifetimes. The troubled boy stomped about cursing.

The circle was not unbroken: many of the faithful of Glad Tidings began to scatter to the four corners, in all likelihood not to preach the gospel, but for some more fundamental reason. Clint, who had broken free from his stepmother, alternated barking and cursing as he approached U-Dean with clenched fists and jerky steps. Aunt Bunch kept her hands over Reverend Buddy's ears, while she hummed "Peace in the Garden."

Several of the elders were tempted to go after the boy, but out of sensitivity for his feelings, perhaps, or more likely because of the desire to defer to the preacher's authority, or for some other reason, they held back and let the boy go on his way. Uncertain whether Clint was coming simply in his general direction or directly at him, U-Dean felt it unnecessary to stand on ceremony and moved toward his truck with speed not evident since his early days in Navy boot camp. Once inside the cab, U-Dean locked the door, hunkered down in his seat, and regarded Clint bobbing his head and cursing all the way out of the parking lot of Glad Tidings.

***

Myrtle McCarty was pissed. She was pissed at that little half-pint preacher, that little sawed-off know-it-all with the squeaky voice who was supposed to help her stepson. She was pissed at that big, heavy woman with dimples smiling like a damned fool and passing around a hat for goodwill offerings. She was especially pissed at the Reverend Armel Armbruster, who didn't have the sense God gave a grapefruit for setting up the whole thing in the first place, or the backbone of an eel for controlling the affair once it got out of hand. And exactly whose big idea was it to have every curiosity seeker and gawker in Southern Maryland there to watch the whole thing?

She was pissed at her late husband Walter for passing in his sleep—just as peaceful as you like—and sticking her with his son, who was as crazy as a catbird. But most of all, she was pissed at herself for ever agreeing to have Clint be the main attraction at a freak show.

With directions strong-armed from the Reverend Armbruster, Myrtle set off with Clint for Lusby to find the Allbrittons. She was going to give each and every last one of them a piece of her mind—a *good* piece of her mind.

Clint was to wait in the car while Myrtle had a "short conversation" with Bunch Allbritton. She banged on the front door, and, after about three minutes, the door cracked and Buddy appeared. It was casual Friday for Buddy: he was wearing a white shirt with blue jeans. The boy explained that he was the only one in the house: his aunt was out back tracking down a chicken for tonight's supper. Cousin U-Dean was off at a Texas Hold 'Em tournament in Delaware and might be gone for the next two days or so.

Myrtle was glaring at the child who was looking and not looking at her when Bunch arrived wiping blood from the butchered rooster on her apron. "Oh."

For the next twenty minutes Myrtle tore Bunch up one side and down the other, and the only thing Bunch could offer was a subdued "Yes'um" with downcast eyes. Myrtle wanted to know exactly why the service hadn't been limited to Clint, herself, and the preacher as she thought it would be. She demanded to know why it had slipped Bunch's mind to mention that the minister was all of eight years old! Myrtle wanted to know if Bunch could guarantee that no part of the service would be on radio since she had seen the WST truck in the parking lot. Myrtle then turned her attention to more practical concerns.

"How exactly is my stepson going to get his high school diploma? You don't think he could ever go back to Patuxent High School, do you? *Do you?*"

"Nome."

"Half the families at that church have kids that go to school with Clint. How exactly is he going to graduate from high school?"

"Ms. McCarty, from the bottom of my heart, I'm sorry."

"Sorry's not good enough, sister. I want to know how Clint's going to finish high school. I promised his father that if he died before me I'd see Clint through high school at least. I want to know how in God's good name I'm going to be able to keep my word?"

Up to this point in her forty-eight years, Bunch Allbritton had never really experienced "wrath" until that day, but afterwards, whenever the seven deadly sins would be discussed in Sunday School and the topic of "wrath" treated, Bunch always pictured the truculence in Myrtle's face and her blazing gray eyes.

"How do I keep my word, sister?"

Bunch explained that she was a certified teacher, that she was already home-schooling Buddy, and that Clint was welcome to finish his high school work with her.

There was more excoriation of Bunch by Myrtle, but as she concluded, "What else can I do?"

Bunch, in a fleeting moment, was tempted to raise the subject of remuneration for her tutoring services, but she resisted that temptation when she regarded the gray menace in Myrtle's eyes. Bunch decided instead to talk scheduling.

***

Clack. Clack.

"King me!"

"Boy, I didn't see *that* coming."

The first voice was Buddy's. The second was an unfamiliar one.

U-Dean almost dropped his six-pack of Corona longnecks when he entered the back porch: Clint McCarty, the demon-possessed teenager, was playing checkers with Buddy at the card table! Bunch occupied the recliner, reading the fourth chapter of Numbers while Myrtle sat in the rocker knitting.

"What the f…"

Clint's dark eyes locked on U-Dean, who quickly looked away and over at his mother.

"Hi, hon. Say hi to Ms. McCarty."

Myrtle cast a cold eye on U-Dean as she continued knitting.

"Ms. McCarty and I patched things up. I'm going to help Clint get his GED," Bunch chirped. "It's the very least…. And while he's here, Clint's going to help Buddy with his math. Clint gets straight-As. Buddy's gonna be taking a little leave of absence from his ministry until his math scores improve…"

U-Dean slouched from the porch and repaired to his room with a couple of longnecks and the latest "Swimsuit Issue" from *Sports Illustrated*. He removed his neck brace and collapsed on his bed. Life, as U-Dean "Jimmy" Allbritton knew it, was coming to an end. *There was no way that the boy was demon-possessed. He was just some young crazy fool, right?* U-Dean got up and locked his bedroom door as Buddy exulted over another jump. *There was simply no way that the boy sitting on the back porch could be….*

The prayers that the Reverend Buddy had been saying for Clint's deliverance must have redounded to U-Dean, for within two days after Clint began tutoring Buddy, U-Dean's neck injury healed— miraculously. In three days, he was back stocking shelves; within a week, Calvert County Sheriff's Deputies were leading U-Dean away in handcuffs through the front door of Home Depot. It seems that U-Dean took particular exception to a customer who had asked him, "Hey, Chief, where are you hiding the elbow joints?" O'Malley, U-Dean's supervisor, tried gamely, but fecklessly, to intervene. Both customer and supervisor were prone by the time two security guards finally restrained U-Dean. The offending customer sustained only contusions to his right eye but immediately vowed legal action. O'Malley, on the other hand, suffered a severe concussion for which he was rushed to Calvert Memorial Hospital in Prince Frederick. The last word was that O'Malley would start receiving workmen's compensation within the month. Because of his record of violence, U-Dean was denied bail while awaiting trial.

As for Buddy and Clint, they seemed to be good for each other. Clint had not suffered an outburst in public since he had started tutoring Buddy, and Buddy finally got the hang of long division. Both guardians felt it wouldn't hurt either boy to continue the contact for a while even after Clint got his GED and Buddy got a better handle on compound fractions. Bunch and Ms. McCarty found that they had a lot in common and thought about liking each other.

There was only one thing left to do: Aunt Bunch, Ms. McCarty, and the boys one rainy afternoon, held hands and prayed over what to do with the donations to the Reverend Buddy Allbritton Outreach program lying idle in an escrow account. After several more days of prayer, it became clear to Bunch that the Lord wanted her to send a money order in the amount of $3,789.67 to St. Jude Children's Hospital, which she did the following day.

But things in life change, and they're never as neat as they are in a story.

The Friday before Labor Day, as the McCartys were leaving, Clint removed his orange and black Baltimore Orioles cap and plopped it on Buddy's head.

"Here, shortstop. Football season's coming. Got to wear my Ravens hat."

Buddy watched Clint walk stiffly out to the car. He wouldn't turn around to wave. He never did. As Buddy watched them drive away, he felt an ache—a deep and lonely feeling—and he didn't understand why. He told Aunt Bunch he didn't feel all that good and wanted to go to bed early. She felt his forehead and observed that he *did* feel a little warm. Buddy was wearing Clint's Orioles cap when he slipped under the covers.

He tried not to remember what Aunt Bunch had predicted that morning: soon the sun would be setting earlier and earlier, and not too much longer the maple leaves would be piled in deep drifts along the walkway out front. He tried not to think that soon Clint might be getting his GED and not long afterwards, leave and never come back. He knew that in time U-Dean would get out of jail and be back home and that the Reverend Buddy Allbritton's sabbatical would finally be over: before he knew it he would be back in the pulpit or in the revival tents or on the airwaves.

For the time being, though, Buddy closed his mind to all that, slid his thumb between his lips, recited the books of the Bible, as he fell asleep picturing a tall dark-eyed boy in a white robe smiling and walking across the waves while he beckoned to Buddy to take his hand.

About the author:

"The Boy Who Walked on Water" marks the third publication for Dan Sullivan. His story "Worthy of Wages" was his first story to be published, appearing as the third place winner in the World Wide Writers' July 2000 contest. (That British publication has since been subsumed under Writers' Forum.) His story "Free Money" appeared in the New Millennium Writings' July 2004 issue. Dan hopes to have one or two more stories published before he seeks an agent who would be willing to market a collection of stories he has been working on for the last eight years or so. Dan is the proud husband of Supawadee, the proud father of Laura and Mark, a pushover for his granddaughters--Kyleigh and Erica, and the fond stepfather of Ploy. He feels privileged to be teaching the terrific students in the Honors British Literature class and the Junior Nonfiction classes at St. Mary's Ryken High School in Leonardtown, Maryland.

~~THIRD PLACE~~

NO LIBRARY CARD
©2007 by Gillian Hamer

That nasty bitch threw me outta the library again. Just 'cos I'm homeless, yer know. She thinks that just 'cos I'm a bum I dunno how ta read. Or maybe she just thinks that I don't have a right ta read. Me body odour might waft down the aisle and bother someone more important than me. P'raps I might even scare a kiddie who is pickin' out some picture books. The big, homeless boogey man lurkin' in the shelves, just waitin' to pounce, yer know. P'raps I'll go on a rampage, rippin' up the books and that. Or p'raps I'll steal 'em, as if sellin' books would get me anythin' anyway. Maybe a couple of dollars at the book exchange. Hardly worth me while is it? She just hates me and she's got the devil's eyes when she looks at me. She's nice as pie ta everyone else who comes in. Me mother always said you can't trust somebody that's got two faces. That's a good way ta describe this library lady, yer know. I should shout it outside the library for everyone to hear it.

"Beware the Two Faced Library Lady! She talks ta homeless people like they're pond scum or somethin'!"

And we're not. I'm not. She deserves to be shamed, yer know.

"If you don't have a library card, you cannot be in the library, sir." She said it ta me all snooty, yer know, like she can't believe she has ta deal with folk such as me.

"Alright then," I says. "Give us a library card then, please, Missus."

"Do you have I.D. with your name and street address on it, sir?" She practically spits out the 'sir' bit of the sentence. She doesn't think I'm much of a sir at all, and she knows very well what me situation is.

"I'm 'omeless love. 'Course I got no I.D.," I whisper, tryin' ta be friendly and that. I even give her a bit of a smile ta break the ice between us.

"No I.D., no library card. No library card, no use of the library. I must ask you to leave, sir, or I will call the police."

The pretty, young assistant librarian looks at me from the corner of her eye. I can see that she pities me and it's embarassin' to say the least, yer know. So I go all red and shuffle out as quickly as me gammy leg will carry me.

Truth is, I don't like ta read that much anyway. I used ta do a bit of readin' in school. Even some Dickens and that. Some days I'll read the papers that are left on the benches at King's Cross Station. It's hard though, yer know. When yer don't have a home ta call yer own and yer a slave ta the bottle, scholastic endeavours can sometimes take a back seat. That's not ta say I'm not smart, yer know. Obviously I got a brain in me head if I can come out with phrases like 'scholastic endeavours'. It's just that me brain gets muddled with the grog, and it's impossible ta hold down a job when yer drunk a lot of the time.

I don't bother nobody. I'm not an abusive drunk or nothin' like that. I wouldn't say boo ta a fly in fact, yer know. But I'm still not fit ta work, so Centrelink says and I agree with 'em. I prefer a drifter lifestyle ta one cooped up in a flat or a boardin' house. Too many people around, watchin' what I'm doin' and that. It makes me nervous, yer know.

I used ta stay in a boardin' house and it was full of lonely, old drunks. It made me really bloody sad. One of 'em, a nice guy called Georgie, he slashed his wrists in the shower. Couldn't take it all anymore. It was fuckin' heartbreakin', yer know. It was only the next day we found out he had a daughter. We thought he had no one. Georgie hadn't spoken ta this daughter of his for nine years. When she got there she just sat outside the place the whole day cryin'. I guess she realised how much time had been wasted and she probably wished things had turned off different, yer know. The sadness that settled on me soul that day was a bit much, so I moved on and haven't slept under a roof since. These days I'm getting' to be an old drunk like Georgie was, but I prefer ta be as free as a bird, yer know.

So why do I feel like I need to be visitin' the library then, yer know? I often wonder this. More than anythin' I think I just like the library for the warmth and the memories. It beckons me with welcomin' arms (well, until the bitch librarian chases me out, that is, yer know). The rows and rows of books invite yer ta lose yerself. Yer wander up and down the aisles breathin' in the musty odours, runnin' yer fingertips along cracked, witherin' spines, and flickin' through yellow, worn pages that are rough ta touch. There are some books in the library that haven't been picked out in years and years. They've been sittin' on the same shelf gatherin' dust, just beggin' for someone ta pick 'em up and discover the secrets of what's inside of 'em. I like to be the person who chooses 'em, 'cos they're the unpopular ones, kind of like me, yer know.

There's also other books there that never seem ta even get back on the shelf, yer know. People put themselves on a waitin' list just ta read 'em. They're usually the newish ones. Flashy, colourful covers. Picture of a trendy, good lookin' writer just inside the cover. They're usually about sex or violence and whatnot, yer know.

Yer might be wonderin' how I know all these things. 'Specially since I don't get past the door nine out of the ten times I try ta enter the library. Well, it's 'cos I used ta work in one. I started at age twenty and worked in one for three years. I still didn't read much, mostly 'cos it was a university library and I spent most of me time lookin' at the girls. Not in a creepy way or nuthin', yer know. I'd just find 'em pretty and I'd imagine up personalities for 'em. I'd be there puttin' books back, lookin' through the shelves for the right number and there a pretty girl would be, cranin' her neck over some lecture notes or a text book. I'd start wonderin' what her name was, what she might be studyin', whether she would have a boyfriend and what colour knickers she had on. I could whittle away hours just like that, dreamin' up ways to start up a conversation. Impress her with some funny comment or say somethin' interestin' about the book she was readin'. I never could think of anythin' witty or interestin', but.

And I was way too shy. I'm still way too shy for me own good, even ta this day, yer know. Of course me chances of scorin' a girlfriend now are even more distant, what with bein' homeless and smelly and an alcoholic with a gammy leg and all. Still, a man can dream, yer know.

Back in me library days it got ta the point where my admirin' glances got noticed and a couple of the girls started ta complain ta the head librarian. They called it leerin' or some such bullshit word. It's not like I was a pervert or anythin' like that. It didn't matter, but. They told me ta find work elsewhere. It's a shame 'cos I really liked that job, yer know. A couple of times when I was stackin' books on Level Three I would kind of be in this girl's way. Her name was Cynthia and when I'd move ta make room, I'd sometimes get a bit of a smile from her, yer know. I reckon if I was there long enough she might have asked me out. She was a sweet, little thing and seemed nice and that, yer know. She would have ta have been the one ta ask me out though of course, yer know, 'cos even the few smiles I got made me just about shit me pants.

I think about Cynthia sometimes. We might have been married with some teenage kiddies by now if things hadn't kind of gone wrong for me. Probably not though. I'm too much of a coward, yer know.

Females are fuckin' nerve wrackin' I can tell yer that much. I never quite have ever managed ta get a girlfriend. A few of the workin' girls on the Cross have offered ta make a man outta me, so to speak, yer know. They purposely call things out to me 'cos they know I go all red and that. They're nice enough girls, doin' it tough, but I'm too timid for anythin' like that. And I got morals about love, yer know. Yer shouldn't just use people if yer don't care, yer know. Yer gotta want ta love someone to treat 'em right. Not that I'm an expert or nothin'. Even if a girl did ask me out, I dunno where I'd take 'er. Not just 'cos I'm broke and alcoholic and that, but 'cos I don't know what girls like ta do. I'd probably take her ta the pictures, 'cos then I wouldn't have ta talk all that much. I could buy her a Coke and some popcorn to show her that I'm nice, and maybe hold her hand if she wanted to.

Anyway, those are just dreams, yer know. No girl wants ta go out with an alco vagrant, especially not an ugly one like me. P'raps if I had nicer teeth it might be okay. I dunno. Maybe not.

So, instead of takin' a pretty girl ta the pictures, I buy a bottle of cheap grog and I take meself inta a back alleyway ta drown me sorrows. Not that I really feel sorry for meself or anything, yer know. I'm okay with everything. Such is life, I think is the sayin' ta use. I like that sayin'. I think it a lot when things make me a bit sad and that. It helps to stay positive, yer know. I put the bottle up ta me lips and let the familiar burn of alcohol slip down me throat. I drink and I drink and I drink and I drink. I drink until me stomach oozes warmth and the cold, dark street around me goes all blurry. I fall asleep and I think about girls. I think about grog. I think about books. And I think about the cosy, warm library, which I have always loved and where I have never been allowed ta belong.

About the author:

As a child Gillian wrote non-stop but this ceased while she was caught in the tangled academic web of high school and university. Gillian has been writing short stories for a year now and hopes to begin a novel in 2007. Her hobbies include reading incessantly, writing, cinema, festivals (film and music), pranks in the workplace, people watching and the beach. Gillian's other short stories include "Dodgy Kebab," "Superheroes of Lunacy," "Gecko," "Stutter Bug," "Brisbane Bogan," and "Van Sadness." Her contact email is gill_22_1999@yahoo.co.uk.

SEA FEVER
©2007 by Rebecca Barton

I must go down to the seas again, to the lonely sea and the sky,
And all I ask is a tall ship and a star to steer her by;
And the wheel's kick and the wind's song and the white sail's shaking,
And a grey mist on the sea's face, and a grey dawn breaking.

I must go down to the seas again, for the call of the running tide
Is a wild call and a clear call that may not be denied;
And all I ask is a windy day with the white clouds flying,
And the flung spray and the blown spume, and the sea-gulls crying.

I must go down to the seas again, to the vagrant gypsy life,
To the gull's way and the whale's way, where the wind's like a whetted knife;
And all I ask is a merry yarn from a laughing fellow-rover,
And quiet sleep and a sweet dream when the long trick's over.
"Sea Fever" by John Masefield, 1900

That poem, written in a flowing but steady hand on an old, yellowed parchment, is hanging in a cracked frame next to the weather-beaten door that leads to the sea. It has hung there for many decades and has set a longing in the hearts of the countless lodgers who have dwelt for a time, long or short, within my four walls. Nestled neatly by those famous white cliffs in Dover I sit, overlooking the sea from what has been called, in the local papers, "a pleasant distance." Pleasant the distance may be to the lodgers here, but to me the space seems a vast expanse; a veritable ocean of sand separates me from that for which I long: the sea itself. In my earlier years, when my hinges did not creak and my paint did not crackle and peel, I used to feel, in a strong storm or at a particularly high tide, that I could almost reach out and touch the sea—but, alas, I never could. When the wind whips up in the night and blows as if to tear my very shingles off, I shudder with desire for the sea. When the rain comes and pours and pelts, I cry a remorseful tear for the ocean which I have never tasted and the joy of the sea which I have never known. For years I have sat here, overlooking that vast blue expanse, yet never able to reach it, never able to fulfill the longing, never able to answer the call of the sea. I know the sea better than any man alive, for it has been my constant companion since the day I was first built. I live by the throb of the sea. I am intimately familiar with all its comings and goings—its caprice, its wild fury, and also its ability to tenderly comfort. For the sea calls me as strongly as it ever called any human man. I have seen many men, rich and poor, happy and sad, who all alike have, in their very nature, a love and desire for the sea which can never be fully quenched.

Some men come to me for health, peace, and rest. Others come for excitement and adventure. But whatever their purpose in coming here, they are all equally called by the sea—either to discover and tame it, or to simply learn to live in harmony with it. So many lodgers pass through my welcoming doors that I could not possibly remember the individual stories of each. But however varied their backgrounds, they all gather here for the same reason: they cannot resist the call of the sea. There are, however, a few particular stories that have always remained with me and which the years do not seem to diminish. One couple I especially remember, for they seemed to have an innocent love of my simple white-washed siding, the smell of the salt sea, and the plaintive cry of the gull that was sincere and deep. Not long after I had been built (maybe a year or two lacking the turn of the century), two prominent English families happened to lodge here at the same time. As was the case with most rich families of the period, the adults did not see their responsibility as parents to be best friends with their children, but instead rather distant, though encouraging, role models. Thus, the only children of these two families, by happenstance a young man and a young lady, were all but left to themselves during their stay. These two young people, whose names I cannot recall, would often take lonely walks by the beautiful shore. After a while, they naturally became acquainted through the manner used by so many romance novelists of being "much thrown together." Having no one else companionable to turn to in their hours of leisure, they soon fell deeply in love, and, to escape their inquisitive parents' notice, often sneaked out at night to meet each other on the lonely beach with the ocean stretched out before them, lit only by the quivering light of a pale moonbeam. When the two families of these loving, though perhaps unwise, young people found out about their children's amours, they were not completely pleased. However, the parents allowed the two lovers to marry, and I had the joy of seeing the couple come back for their honeymoon. If I remember correctly, they even came back for a third visit, this time with a child of their own. This couple discovered that the call of the sea is a beautiful call; for the ocean, though terrible in its wrath and threatening in its grumblings, is altogether irresistibly lovely. This couple came back to this spot where they first met, not only because of the memories that are held here, but because the memories themselves were made the more sacred and the more dear for being formed by the sea. They could not resist its call.

One other lodger here I remember particularly, a young wife, who came here not long after the First World War. A beautiful young woman who was full of life and vigor, she had a sparkle about her that I have rarely beheld in any other person. She came here in advance of her husband, who was sailing in the next day. He was coming in after a long trip to France on some business or other and was to join her here. She spent many happy hours down by the sea, staring across the glittering ocean which was to carry her husband home, all the while dreaming of their future life together. However, that night, a large storm blew in, and during the night, the young husband's boat foundered upon the rocky shore, killing all who were onboard. The young widow was completely distraught. She had no relatives to whom to turn, and her husband left her very little money. My landlord at the time had not the heart to turn her out, and so he kept the young widow on as a helper and cook, by which employment she earned her room and board. One might have thought that staying in the same house and by the same shore where she first heard of her dear husband's death would hold too many painful memories to be a pleasant life. However, when she had stayed for several years and had earned enough money to be able to go out on her own, she did not take the chance to leave this house by the shore, preferring to stay on and work by the sea. Her story reveals another side of the sea: its ability to comfort. Though pain and sorrow may be closely related to it for whatever reason, the sea is still able to calm and soothe the soul. When many years are spent in the ocean's company, it becomes a friend to the weary and a comforter to those who mourn. Accordingly, this young widow found peace in taking lonely walks by the sea or simply standing and letting the sea spume wash away her tears in its reassuring bath. She, too, could not resist the sea's call.

There is yet another memory that will be difficult to relate, as the subject touches me so deeply and strikes me so hard at the very core of my longing. Not many years ago now, an old retired navy captain came to lodge here for reasons of his bad health. The doctors did not expect that he should live long. He had fought in both World Wars, and he had earned many medals for bravery and dedication. The sea was his life; from the time he was a small boy, he had loved ships and sailing, and when he was old enough, he ran away from home to enter the Navy. Now old and frail, he was hardly able to roll himself in his wheeled chair across the beach so that he could look for a few last times upon the sea which had, for his whole life, been his constant companion. The ocean was his friend, as well as his enemy. The old captain knew the destructive power and malice of the sea, and yet he had spent so much time sailing the ocean the world over that he had learned to harness that teeming strength and use it for his own purposes. Now that he was incapacitated, the captain experienced a growing frustration with his limited freedom, both physical and mental. The doctors would not tell him the seriousness of his case, but the captain knew his danger instinctively. Every day seemed to bring him lower and to send him into deeper levels of despondency. The old captain's only happy hours were those he spent in the company of the ocean, gazing across its deceptive yet familiar face until the evening grew too dark and a nurse came to fetch the captain and take him inside. After several days in which the old man worsened rapidly and was confined to his bed, he seemed to take a turn for the better. The doctors acquiesced to his wishes to be taken out to the cliffs and allowed to sit there, undisturbed, until the sun set. I watched him sadly and almost fondly, for I felt we had something in common. Neither of us could freely go to the sea as we both wished—the sea sighed, and the sea called, but we could not answer. As I watched the captain sitting by the sea, I saw him, through some enormous strength of effort, stand up, lean perilously for a moment or two upon his chair, and at last throw himself, in a final gesture of defiance, into the sea. His death was sadly mourned by all who knew him, and a beautiful funeral was held by the sea. The old captain, at the last, could not resist its call. May I be allowed to say that I envied him?

I should like to know that when my life is utterly spent, and my timbers are cracked, and my windows broken, that I, too, may throw myself into the sea and quench, as though putting out a flame, my burning desire to answer the sea. For, when the end of all things comes, and this world is passing, the sea shall engulf me, and I, too, will no longer be able to resist the sea's call.

About the author:

Rebecca Barton is currently a freshman at Houston Baptist University pursuing a degree in Business. She was home schooled from kindergarten through high school which gave her unique opportunities to explore her own personal talents and areas of interest. Rebecca's family spent part of her childhood living in Wales and England, and from there she had the chance to travel across much of Europe. She enjoys discovering interesting movies and rereading favorite books. She also appreciates music of many different genres, playing both the piano and the cello and participating in her college choir. Rebecca dabbles in creative photography, and she loves the rain.

GOODBYE MY SWEET
©2007 by Kathryn Mattingly

Gino watched her silver sports car swing into the scenic pullout and come to a stop not far from his beater truck. Long slender legs exited first from the open door, causing his libido to kick into overdrive. With a wicked grin, Tessa approached him and they locked into a kiss that only hinted of the passion yet to unfold in the bushes nearby.

But not tonight, he had to remind himself, although it was difficult to bypass the pleasures of her body as he caressed a bare midriff exposed beneath a tiny halter-top. He longed to run a hand up her thigh beneath the flowery short skirt, but thought better of it. Gino didn't want anything to sway his determination. His plan was set. He need only follow it to the letter and not let his testosterone sabotage it.

"Just one more week, Gino, and we're out of here forever," Tessa whispered in his ear.

Gino hugged her close and cupped her tight little bottom. He gruffly whispered back, "Tessa, did you get the bag of old coins from the rock yet?" He kissed the top of her hair and tried not to think about how sweet she smelled.

"No," she sighed, her head buried in his shoulder.

"Why not?" he asked annoyed.

Tessa pulled back to look at him. "It's not that easy. I forgot how silly we were to hide them on the other side of the rock wall. I mean, we were just kids, and now the thought of climbing over those old wobbly stones seems impossible."

"Tessa, we can't leave the bag of coins. It's worth a small

fortune." Gino tried not to sound overly disappointed that the treasure wasn't in her possession, sitting in that sixty thousand dollar sports car just waiting for him to shove in his backpack.

He thought of the legend suggesting the coins stolen by pirates of long ago brought immortality to whoever possessed them. Just what he needed, more than one lifetime of knowing Tessa didn't love only him. Such reality was too brutal to consider, yet it didn't stop him from wanting to steal back the priceless coins he had given her as a young boy sick with puppy love.

Gino wondered if he should postpone his plan, but decided that wasn't possible. This was their last rendezvous by the overhang. He'd have no other opportunity to do what he felt was justified…hell, was necessary. He pulled her to him, kissing those sensual lips long and hard and thought about when they were just kids. He had fallen so deeply in love with her that it hurt. It still hurt, but not nearly as much as when he first realized what a fool he had been to think he was the only guy in her life. Why hadn't he noticed the lustful eyes of other fieldworkers sooner? Those few big dark-haired blokes like himself that Tessa always brought water and sandwiches to?

He moved his hands up along the shape of her body, felt her full breasts in the braless halter-top one last time, and finally rested them on her delicate neck. His fingers touched the raven hair caressing her shoulders. He ran them through the silky locks as he recalled how wildly excited he had been that day he found the bag of coins. It was in the overgrown vineyard, where they had sent him to cut firewood. Always working when you're a vineyard peasant, he thought, while the owner's kid swam in their private pool and sipped lemonade. But Gino was never resentful until now. He just liked getting a glimpse of Tessa, dreaming that she'd notice him one day.

And then he found the leather bag when pulling up an old shriveled vine. Filled with treasure, it was. Big round heavy coins from a time and place far removed. Even at twelve he knew that. But only recently had they discovered what the coins were worth, and how the pirates had hidden them in the San Francisco Bay. Rumor had it that someone in the Sorrentino lineage had been a pirate, and brought part of the treasure to the Napa Valley when starting a vineyard here. Gino didn't care if Tessa came from pirates or not. All he cared about was that she want only him, which she didn't.

He tightened his grip on her lovely neck, but she failed to notice.

She was busily untying his belt until finally one velvet hand slipped beneath his bellybutton and headed seductively for those pulsing nether regions. He had to quit stalling. In one mighty thrust he lifted her by the neck and pushed her over the railing, watching the puzzled eyes for an instant as she fell down and down, and then down some more into the deep ravine. The Napa River merely trickled along its way here, groping silently past sheer canyon walls until reaching a spot at which it would widen and deepen. He knew that's where they'd find her body, after they discovered her fancy car up at this pullout and pieced it all together.

"Goodbye, my sweet," he called to her, as she nearly reached the bottom. If he were lucky, they'd believe she jumped. Worse case scenario, someone would recognize his beater truck. Then he'd have to lie. *I broke up with her and we parted ways. She must've been more upset than I realized to jump like that. I should've never left her there all alone....*

He hoped he could make himself seem choked up if it came to that. And he would be, of course, because he loved her with all of his heart, which had made the thought of sharing her with other men unbearable. And then there was the fact of how she was using him to get away, to escape her tyrannical father and be free at last to do as she pleased. Gino understood finally how he was merely her ticket out, her transportation to Italy, where he still had family they could stay with. But even there, Tessa would find other men to flirt with.

A few weeks later, Gino stood perfectly still as the long procession of cars made their way slowly down the private road. They had emerged from the mansion where Tessa was laid out in a closed casket, after her remains had been discovered in the Napa River, where it swells at the end of the steep canyon. He stared at the rows and rows of straight fertile grape vines waving gently in the breeze beyond the cars, and tried to ignore the tears he couldn't seem to stop for his sweet dead Tessa, whom he'd always love.

He wished she'd felt the same, wished she hadn't pushed him to do such a desperate thing, but he'd rather have her dead than share her. Gino glanced at his peers, their sweat soaked bodies erect as the line of vehicles went by. He tried not to notice those few young bucks that Tessa had taken a liking to.

No one asked him about the incident on the scenic pullout where Tessa had fallen to her death. It was assumed that she had jumped. No one knew why, but they suspected her demanding father had laid the law down about her spending time with his laborers, instead of those more appropriate young suitors from neighboring vineyards. Such an argument with her old man, combined with the discovery of her pregnancy, still hidden in its first stages, would explain jumping to her death. Gino didn't know for a fact that Tessa had been unfaithful to him, but he hated how she made him suspect it nonetheless.

Much to Gino's relief, after every last grape was picked, the field hands received their annual invitation to the Harvest Celebration on the grounds behind the mansion, despite the close proximity in time to Tessa's death. Tradition had it that when the harvest was in, hired hands could eat, drink, and dance to their hearts' content. He would find a way to sneak over to the far side of the grounds where he and Tessa had shimmied up the old stonewall and shoved the bag of coins in a space between two mortared rocks on the other side.

As luck would have it, the young homeless girl sheltered by the Sorrentinos shortly after Tessa's death had taken a shining to him. The child looked to be no more than ten to Gino, and stuck to him like glue from the moment he arrived and gulped down his first glass of tart new wine.

"What's your name?" she asked, staring up at him with a shy grin.

"Gino," he smiled back, recalling how this little Jasmine had awakened among the grapevines in the upper field, and then walked along the rows of grapes until someone approached her. She was dazed and dirty, hair all stringy and clingy to her tear-stained face. She claimed not knowing who she was. One of the field men took her to the big house on the hill. Before anyone knew anything, Mrs. Sorrentino had taken her in and given her a name and bedroom just down the hall from where Tessa had slept. Authorities were looking for leads but so far, nothing. And now here she was sticking to Gino like a fly on a horse's back.

"What's your name?" he asked, already knowing, but letting on like he didn't.

"Jasmine. At least now it is. I don't know what it was before," she answered, without the least bit of remorse. "Miss Lydia says I'm like a breath of fresh air in the house, that I remind her of the jasmine bushes in her garden." Jasmine's eyes sparkled. "Their tiny pink buds are the first sign she has of spring."

"Is that right?" Gino asked, thinking that Tessa's mom, whom

Jasmine referred to as Miss Lydia, must surely be desperate for a reason to live, since her beautiful daughter was dead. He could only hope the money from selling the old coins would help him lick his wounds of lost love for the next fifty years.

Gino recalled a time long ago when he had first decided to give his newly found treasure to Tessa. All he could think about was how pleased she would be, and how he'd finally stand out from the other boys who worked the fields.

As Jasmine rattled on about unimportant things, his mind escaped back to that first kiss. It was on the cheek. Tessa was very pleased indeed with his gift. Her little cherry lips had grinned seductively, despite her only being eleven. Those clear blue eyes had penetrated his own until he had to look away for fear that she would read his thoughts, and know how much he wanted her for his own, even then.

"Wanna go for a walk?" the child asked, bringing Gino back to the present. He thought for a minute, and then responded yes indeed, he did want to go for a walk. Perhaps this little cherub from nowhere would be helpful in retrieving Tessa's bag of coins. He could buy Jasmine's silence by giving her one.

Hand in hand they crossed through flowering bushes and fields of grass, all the while Gino thinking how perfect to have the child as an excuse for his wandering. Soon, they reached the stonewall that ran across the property line to the front of the vineyard. He could almost hear his and Tessa's voices of long ago as they hid the leather pouch in a place impossible for anybody to stumble upon.

Jasmine," he began, "a long time ago, when I was your age, I used to come here with Tessa. Do you know who Tessa was?"

"Of course," Jasmine offered up. "That's the lady who drowned in the river before I came." She grinned widely and Gino thought for an instant she resembled the beautiful dead Tessa with her full red lips and raven hair. He felt another twinge of regret for the way things had turned out. It seemed not long ago that he and Tessa herself had stood here and contemplated climbing this wall, with the ravine far below precariously awaiting a single slip on the other side.

"She was Miss Lydia's little girl," Jasmine added, her grin reduced now to a coy smile, her eyes slightly saddened but still bright and blue. Gino was suddenly struck by the attractiveness and endearing nature of this sweet, homeless creature. Perhaps he should have paid more attention to all that she rambled on about earlier. It might have helped him understand her better, for certainly she was no simpleton. His curiosity about Jasmine was growing steadily by the minute.

Gino knelt beside her and spoke softly. "Well, I found some buried treasure one day, right here on this estate. A leather bag filled with some old coins. I gave it to Tessa. We climbed this wall and halfway down the other side to shove it into a space between two stones for safekeeping. But now I'm too big and the wall may not hold my weight."

He paused and let this information sink into her pretty head.

"I see. Well, is the treasure still there?" she asked sweetly, while staring at the wall and cupping her eyes from the sun.

"I believe it is. At least, I hope it is," Gino answered. "If you're brave enough to shimmy over this wall for me, I'll give you one of the coins in the bag."

"Really? To keep?"

"Absolutely."

"Cross your heart and hope to die?"

"Cross my heart and hope to die." Gino made the heart crossing gesture with his right hand.

"Okay! Let's do it!" Needing no further encouragement, Jasmine began to climb the wall with Gino right behind her. When they reached the top, both stared silently at the canyon below. A breeze cooled their hot faces. Sounds of rushing water were all they could hear. It drowned out the laughter and music from the party on the other side of the manicured grounds.

"It's scary up here," Jasmine admitted, glancing behind her at Gino.

"There's nothing to be afraid of." He shouted above the wind and rushing water echoing up the canyon. "Let me see if I can reach far enough over," he suggested, moving along beside Jasmine. He straddled the wall, little stones and old mortar falling away as he did so. Carefully, Gino lowered his body onto the other side, thinking Tessa had been wrong. It wasn't hard to do at all, no harder than the effort he made to put the pouch between the rocks in the first place.

Jasmine rested her arms on top of the wall and watched him, her blue eyes filled to the brim with admiration for his bravery. Ever so carefully, he reached down and groped the stones that surely held the coins wedged between them. Soon, he felt the leather pouch! Barely able to grip it, Gino slowly tugged until it came free. He stood back up and showed the bag to his new little friend. Jasmine giggled gleefully and clapped her hands. But then a rock slipped from beneath Gino's feet and he had to hang on for dear life, tossing the bag to Jasmine.

"Hold the treasure tightly," he instructed while concentrating his efforts solely on climbing back over to safety.

"No problem," Jasmine answered. "It is, after all, *my* treasure," she added, while pushing him mightily with all her weight. Teetering for an instant on the edge of the wall, Gino stared at Jasmine. Something about her was so familiar, as if those clear blue eyes reached all the way to another soul…all the way to Tessa. Yes, it was his Tessa that he saw there in those eyes, as he lost his foothold and tumbled to his death.

"Goodbye, my sweet," he heard the child say as he fell down and down, and then down some more to the rushing Napa River below. His final thoughts were not of his undying love for Tessa, but about the legend of immortality for whoever possessed the coins.

It must have been true after all.

About the author:

Kathryn Mattingly lives in El Dorado Hills, CA. She has a fine arts degree from the University of Oregon, and an MAT from Pacific U. Kathryn developed and teaches an after school art enrichment program called Angelo Art. She is also a private tutor for kindergarten through third grade students struggling with reading skills, and for fourth through eighth grade students gifted in creative writing. A six time Maui Writers attendee, she has worked under various accomplished authors including: Terry Brooks, Elizabeth George, Dorothy Allison, John Saul, and Gail Tsukiyama. Her goal is to be a published novelist, and therefore Kathryn is happy to have a NY agent at JCA Literary Agency representing her last manuscript, currently being considered for publication. To date, Kathryn has twelve anthology and magazine publications, and has won recognition for several of her short pieces of fiction. Two of her stories are in current anthologies: *Womanscapes* (Amazon.com) and *Award Winning Stories* (joyuspub.com).

FINDING LOVE AND EMPLOYMENT AFTER FORTY

©2007 by Ranae Cherry

Chapter One

"Rebecca…we…. need to talk." Robert announced.

"I've made your favorite dinner, let me fix you a drink and meet you in the dining room."

The table was set, the candles were lit, and she was wearing her sexiest dress with pearls, her dark hair pulled back in a French twist. Forty-three years old and still beautiful.

"We need to make some changes, Rebecca."

"Yes, we do. And I think I know why."

"You do?"

"I'm not blind, Robert. After twenty-two years of marriage, you'd think I'd know you by now."

He rolled his eyes and sat down, his head held in his hands.

"Are you okay?" She asked, returning with the Scotch. "Bad day at the office?"

"Rebecca…"

She put down her glass. "Okay, I'm all ears."

He looked into her eyes. "I…want…a divorce."

"What?"

"Becca," he was using her pet name now, "we've been growing apart for a long time…"

He was right. Ever since he'd made partner, they'd taken different paths. While the long hours and weekends were to be expected, and she was busy with designing and overseeing construction of their house and of course raising Alixandra, the years had flown by.

"...I've met someone else. I don't want to hurt you, Becca, it's just we're not the same people anymore. Time does that, I guess."

The walls were closing in all around her. "Anyone I know?"

"Stacy."

Tears were welling up in her eyes, "How long has this been going on?"

"Six months."

Rebecca began pacing the room, "Stacy...she's a twenty-two year old child, for God's sake." Rebecca remembered the long legged beauty from the company picnic.

"She's not a child."

"Our daughter just turned nineteen," Rebecca reached for her drink.

"I didn't ask for this to happen, Becca. I love this woman."

"This is not love, Robert...this is a mid-life crisis." Rebecca drained the last drop from her glass and poured another drink.

"You had better go easy on that stuff."

"Don't..." pointing a finger in his face "...tell me what to do."

"I don't want this to get ugly," he said.

"Excuse me?"

"We should calm down...handle this like adults."

"I wasn't the one cheating...you...over-priced ambulance chaser."

"Let's not call names, shall we? This degrades you."

"Sorry...I must have missed the class on cheating husbands, Etiquette 101."

"I can't talk to you like this." Robert headed for the bedroom where he began packing his bags.

"So that's it." Bringing the bottle with her, "You're going to throw away our marriage over this...talking Barbie doll?"

"There's no point in me staying here. You can reach me on my cell if you need to."

"Twenty-two years of trust shot to hell."

"I've been a good husband."

"Oh the best...you may be difficult to replace."

"We'll talk later...after you've calmed down."

She yelled, "I wouldn't count on it. You may not live that long, dear boy." A thrown vase hit the wall just as he closed the door behind him. "I hope your toupee gets fleas!"

***

For the next year, Rebecca was on automatic pilot, going through the motions of the divorce and selling the 5,000 square foot house she had put so much of herself into.

Her best friend, Sandy, offered her a place to stay at her condo, but Rebecca declined and found a quaint apartment. She had plenty of money from her share of the house and the alimony checks she was granted from the divorce. Money wasn't the issue, just starting her life over was.

Chapter Two

Walking towards her car, Rebecca thought, *Another job bites the dust.*

Having little skills other than her degree in fashion and being a mother, Rebecca didn't know where to begin. She had only worked at various places during the Christmas season which didn't look impressive on a resume. After this last interview, she was on her way to have lunch with Sandy.

As the hostess escorted Rebecca; Sandy said, "Over here." Lighting her cigarette.

Sandy and Rebecca had been best friends all through college and no two could be more opposite. Sandy refused to marry; ever the career girl, she had her own column in the *Columbus Dispatch*. She had one cat named Fuzz Wart and tropical fish, and that was the extent of responsibility Sandy could handle.

Before Rebecca could sit, Sandy asked, "So, how did it go…and what was it for?"

"This was the worst one. This guy kept looking at my chest and he had something green between his two front teeth and pontificated about what he was looking for in a marketing director…then after we were through he said that he would be sure to call me…if he wanted to have a second interview."

"Stuff your bra." Sandy said, taking a puff from her smoke.

"What?"

Leaning over the table, Sandy continued, "Look, I was part of the interviewing process for a new editor at the paper. Well, this one lady about our age came in and was perfect. Hell, she had been the assistant managing editor for the Washington Post—so come on—the woman had the perfect résumé. But this twenty-five year old twit comes in with huge tits, cleavage showing and no experience, and they hired her—against my will, mind you. So play their games and stuff your bra and wear something sexy. You have a cute enough shape to pull it off."

"I'm not going to stuff my bra…that's just wrong. Besides, tomorrow I'm interviewing for an office assistant and the woman I talked with sounded promising."

"Okay…look, all I'm saying is that it's tough out there for someone our age. Everyone wants people between ages twenty and thirty; anyone forty or over can forget it."

"Let's talk about something else."

"Have you heard from Robert?"

"Did you have to bring him up…? I'm depressed enough as it is. And no, not since the sale of our house. I guess he and the newest of the twenty-year-old-club are off on vacation somewhere."

"You should have kept the house."

"I couldn't afford the house. What are you ordering?" Rebecca asked.

"The grilled chicken ceaser salad."

"That sounds good."

After ordering, Sandy lit up another cigarette, causing Rebecca to say, "You should quit smoking…it's not good for you."

"I've cut back, so don't hassle me. Hey! There's a condo for sale in my development. Have you thought about getting out of that apartment?"

"I need to find a job first; and besides, I'm fine where I'm at."

"Are you having desert?"

"I don't think so…just coffee." Rebecca frowned.

"Oh, I forgot to tell you. This gorgeous new writer started Monday. I thought of you. How about joining me and a few of my co-workers for a night out and you two can meet."

"Will you stop trying to set me up? I'm not interested in dating." Finishing her coffee she added, "How about *your* love life."

"There isn't hope for me…I'm too selfish," Sandy smiled.

"Besides, I have Fuzz Wart and the fish."

"Oh, *that* is…exciting."

After lunch the two women went their separate ways.

***

As Rebecca parked in her designated space, she noticed a man getting out of the car next to hers. He was tall, blond hair with a Robert Redford physic about him. She felt embarrassed as he smiled at her so she hurried to her door. It wasn't until the next day that she ran into him again as she was leaving for the interview.

"Hi," he said with a smile that would melt any woman's heart.

"Hello." Taking her keys out, she asked, "Just move in?"

"Yes. Guess we're neighbors…what's your name?"

"Rebecca…and yours?"

"Eric Taylor," he answered, extending his hand to shake hers. "You're the first person I've met here."

"Well…welcome to the neighborhood."

"Thanks. Going to work?" Eric asked.

"I wish. No, going to a job interview."

"Maybe we could get together sometime…being that I don't know much about the area." Flashing an electric smile.

"Sure," Rebecca said as she hurried to her car thinking, *just what I need…a man prettier then me.*

Traffic in Columbus was a real issue at this time in the morning. She was hoping she could find the place with out a problem. Having the directions in her hand and trying to steer with the other while focusing on the road was almost too much. Finally finding the right building, she parked in the company garage.

"May I help you?" The receptionist asked.

"Yes…I'm here for a nine o'clock appointment with Ms. Adams?" Rebecca smiled.

"I'll buzz her. Do you have your résumé?"

"No."

The receptionist gave a slight sigh, handing her a clip board. "Here, fill this out. You can have a seat over there." She pointed towards a small room, which, by this time, was filling in with other possible candidates.

Rebecca scoped out the competition. One girl looked to be in her mid-twenties, very attractive with dyed blond hair, a skin tight suit that revealed an ample bust line and long tan legs.

The next woman waiting was middle-aged with a dark dress and flat shoes, short brown hair with a little gray peaking through. She was reading a magazine and, sitting on the floor next to her feet, was a briefcase probably containing her résumé.

"Ms. Black," the receptionist called. She smiled to the other women waiting, and then escorted Rebecca through the grease-filled plant. She finally led her to the conference room where Rebecca took a seat at the end.

It wasn't long before Ms. Adams came in. Rebecca guessed she was in her sixties, tall, thin with her white hair pulled back. She wore a black suit with a scarf held by a fashionable pin.

"Rebecca Black?" Ms. Adams asked looking over the top of the application she held in her bony hands.

"Yes." She replied, standing to shake the woman's hand.

"Please…sit." Ms. Adams was all business. "This is all of your work experience?"

"Yes…"

"I see here that you only worked retail during the holiday season and not at the same place twice. Why?"

"Well…I guess because when I went to Lazarus the following year they had hired enough to cover the floor so I found that Toys "R" Us was hiring and worked there." Rebecca could see that this woman was not going to give her a chance.

"I see…and what did you do the rest of the time?"

"I used to be married…"

"Oh I see. You're one of those."

"Excuse me?"

"You know…needing a career later in life."

"Look…you can call anyone on that list and you will find that I was a dependable employee."

Looking up at Rebecca, Ms. Adams put down the application, "We need someone to start right away. The hours are full-time and no weekends. The pay starts at eleven dollars an hour, and after you are here ninety days we offer insurance. I will call you and let you know if we are interested—don't call us. Can you find your way out?"

"Yes." Rebecca headed for the door.

Walking through where the other ladies were waiting for their interviews, she paused long enough to say, "Good luck. You'll need it."

Looking at her watch, it was only ten-past-ten. She called Sandy to meet her for lunch. Since she didn't have any other interviews lined up, Rebecca decided to swing by home to change into jeans and a sweater. Pulling into her parking space, she noticed Eric's car was there. *Doesn't he work?*

***

Rebecca saved a booth while waiting for her friend. People were filing in and out as the lunch hour was fast approaching. She watched the "working" people with interest: women in pant suits, dress suits, dresses—some short and sexy, some plain and drab looking; men in suits or in Dockers and sweaters. All of them had one thing in common: they were employed; whether they liked their jobs or not, at least they had one.

Sandy breezed in with her usual high energy level. She always looked great. She gave Rebecca a hug and kiss as she sat across from her. "How did it go this morning?"

"Don't ask."

"That bad? What Troglodyte did you meet today?" Sandy lit up a cigarette.

"Ms. Adams. Don't you remember me telling you about our conversation over the phone when I called for an interview?"

"Oh…yeah…you thought you might have a chance. What in the hell happened?"

"I don't know…she didn't seem to be impressed with my work history. Or me for that matter." Rebecca was thinking about a ham and cheese on rye sounding good.

"Well…what's next in the ongoing quest for finding the right job?"

"I really don't know where to look. Maybe at the mall. I *do* have a degree in fashion."

"Find out what you really want to do and then go for that instead of just trying to find anything. It's not like you need the money."

"That's not the point, Sandy. I want to feel good about myself again. I want to feel like I'm a productive part of society." She felt a tear escaping, knowing there were more to follow once she returned home.

"Hey…what are you doing Sunday?" Sandy changed the subject.

"Nothing that I know of…why?"

"I'm having a little gathering…just a few co-workers and friends…why don't you come?"

"What time?"

"Around one in the afternoon."

"I'll think about it. What should I bring?"

"Make your Mexican Fruit Cake with the cream cheese icing that everyone loves so much."

"I'll call you Saturday and let you know for sure if I'm coming, okay?"

"Sounds good. Now quit feeling sorry for yourself and order." Sandy knew Sunday would be a great time to play cupid and introduce her to the new writer.

"You know Sandy, you missed your true calling. You should have been a therapist with your tender, loving way." Rebecca chided.

The truth was that Sandy was the only true friend Rebecca had left after the divorce. All of the friends she and Robert had made together seemed to side with him and leave her out of everything.

***

The phone rang just as she was settled in her apartment ready to watch *Anywhere but Here*. She paused the movie, "Hello."

"Becca," said Robert.

"Yes."

"I need a ride…my car broke down and I had to have it towed to the garage."

"Can't your latest flame pick you up…or is it past her bed time?"

"Please, Becca. I'll buy you dinner."

"Don't bother. Where are you?"

"At the Volvo dealer off of Morris road."

"Give me twenty minutes."

"Thanks, Becca."

"Call me Rebecca. I don't care for the pet name anymore."

She grabbed her keys and was out the door. She couldn't help notice as she got into her car that Eric's car was gone. *So, he does have a life.*

Robert was standing in front of the dealership. "Thanks, Bec…I mean Rebecca."

"Should I take you home?"

"That would be great." Robert didn't press stopping to get a bite to eat.

He had bought a huge house in Worthington after the divorce. Rebecca guessed he needed to impress Stacy.

"Have you heard from Alix?"

"She called yesterday. Why?" She wanted this drive to be shorter.

"Just wondered. Do you see her much?"

"Not since she left home and started school. How about you?"

"She was here last weekend."

"How will you get your car when it's ready?"

"I have a friend that will take me to pick it up."

"Oh…I don't even want to know." Rebecca held up her hand.

"It's not what you think. A guy at the office."

"I really don't care."

The rest of the ride was silent. As she pulled into the circular driveway, Robert asked, "Want to come in for a drink…or a cup of coffee?"

"No thanks."

"Well…thanks for the ride. I'll call you later in the week. Maybe we could go out for dinner or something."

Rebecca turned to look at her ex-husband. Squinting her eyes, she said, "I don't want a date with you."

As soon as he closed his door, she hit the car in drive, nearly running over his foot.

As she pulled into her parking spot, she noticed Eric's car.

Back in the apartment, she decided it was Friday and she had nowhere else to go after rescuing her ex-husband, so she popped popcorn and settled down on her sofa to watch a movie. She would attend Sandy's brunch, and then start fresh with the job search on Monday.

Chapter Three

The next morning Rebecca woke up to a banging on the door. Looking through the peep-hole, she saw Alix standing with a basket full of dirty clothes.

"Why didn't you use your key?"

"I forgot it at Dad's last weekend. And why aren't you up yet mom? You never sleep past eight." Alix dropped her bags by the staircase.

Rebecca began making coffee and yelled to her daughter, "I must have fallen asleep on the sofa last night while watching a movie." Alix came up behind, giving her a hug, then settled down in one of the chairs. "Are you hungry?" Rebecca asked.

"Not really. Maybe a bagel would be nice." Alix was a girl who could eat anyone out of house and home, and to look at her you would never know it. She was as tall as her father, light blond hair and, inheriting her mother's olive skin, she looked like the Suntan Goddess you see on the big screen. No frills, no fuss, but then she had that rare beauty that didn't need to be accented by the fake bling-bling of society.

"You went to your father's last weekend?"

"I thought I told you. He asked if I could come set up his new lap top. So while I was there I used the indoor pool and decided to stay the weekend. Of course, I didn't know that he would have Bobby Joe there."

"Bobby Joe?"

"The latest kewpie doll. She's is a real hoot, mom…I don't know where he met this one…but I assure you not at a place where she would have to think. To think she is my age just makes me ill."

"I didn't know he was seeing someone else. What happened to Stacy?"

"Oh, you didn't hear." Smiling, Alix continued, "Stacy started seeing one of the new lawyers in Dad's firm. She evidently liked the young, thirty year old fresh out of Yale…so she is now working for the other guy. Poor Dad can't keep up, but at least Stacy was smart. This new one…I don't think Dad will have to worry about another attorney sweeping her off her feet."

"How's Scott?" Rebecca handed Alix her bagel and coffee.

"Good. He's going camping this weekend with some of his friends…and I didn't feel like going."

"Are you two that serious?"

"Well…we have discussed living together, because as I told you on the phone my roommates are driving me crazy and I need my space. But I'm not sure that I'm ready to make that kind of commitment just yet...you know?"

"I really think you should be married before living with a man."

"Yeah...and where did it get you, mom?"

"Alix."

"Come on, mom. I'm not getting married. Living together is like test driving before you buy."

"I'm not having this conversation this early in the morning."

"So...what are you doing this weekend?"

"Nothing much. Tomorrow I'm going to Sandy's for brunch. Do you want to come with me?"

"Not really...but thanks. I'll just hang around here studying and do my laundry."

The rest of the day was uneventful. Rebecca ran a few errands, shopping, and baking her Mexican Fruit cake. Alix stayed around the apartment. It was nice having someone there.

"Hey, mom, who is your new neighbor? You know...the cute blond."

"Eric Taylor...why?" Rebecca was busy making taco salads for dinner.

"Just curious. I saw him going to the mail box."

"Don't go there, Alix...you sound like Sandy."

Rebecca and Alix enjoyed their evening, watching movies and relaxing. Sunday morning, Rebecca decided to dress in her favorite suit. Packing up the cake, grabbing her purse and keys, she was heading out the door as Eric was walking towards his car.

"Good-morning, Rebecca," Eric greeted her with a smile.

"Hello."

"Where are you off to looking gorgeous?"

"To brunch." As a last minute thought she asked, "Would you care to join me?"

Eric smiled, "Sure...why not? I was going to play a little racquetball but I'll call and cancel since your invitation sounds more fun."

"I don't want to ruin your plans?"

"You're not. I'll call him on the way. Should I drive or do you want to?"

"I'll drive since I know the way."

"Is what I'm wearing okay?"

"Perfect."

Rebecca thought the man could wear a brown sack and look great, but his jeans and sweater worked just fine. Once in the car, Eric made his phone call. He turned to Rebecca flipping his phone off, "So...where does your friend live and how long have you known her?"

"She lives in Dublin."

"Oh."

Traffic was beginning to pick up pace with people getting out of church. Rebecca felt awkward during the drive, not knowing what to say and she was beginning to think this was a mistake to have invited him.

Cars were slowing to a crawl, giving the two of them time to talk.

"How long were you married?" Eric asked, finding her a bit mysterious.

"Is it that obvious?" she sighed. "Seems like forever."

"What's forever?"

"Twenty-two years."

"Any kids?"

"We have a daughter...twenty...going to Ohio State." Rebecca then asked, "And you? Ever married, any kids?"

Traffic was beginning to move a little faster now.

"Never married. I *do* have a cat. Does that count?"

"What's your cat's name?"

"Fluffy."

Rebecca laughed, "Fluffy...he sounds ferocious."

"She can be."

They chuckled as Rebecca turned into the entrance of Sandy's development. "This is it."

"Nice place...what does your friend do?"

"She's a journalist, and one of the editors for the Columbus Dispatch; been there since she graduated from college."

Sandy opened the door, hugging Rebecca, then stepping back to look over the tall wonder standing beside her. "And who is this cool drink of water?" Sandy asked, smiling to her best friend.

"Eric...Sandy...Sandy...Eric...my neighbor," smiled Rebecca.

"Well...well...well. *Now* I see why you aren't anxious to move. Come in...make yourself at home...stay as long as you like." Sandy winked towards Eric.

Rebecca gave Sandy a friendly glare.

Sandy directed Eric towards the kitchen, saying, "Help yourself to anything in here." In a seductive tone she continued with "Food...drinks...whatever. I need to borrow Rebecca for just a minute."

Rebecca looked around, noticing the animal print décor throughout the condo. It had been some time since she had been by.

"Come back to my bedroom for a minute...I want you to see my new comforter and dressing table." Sandy grabbed Rebecca's arm.

She closed the door behind them; Rebecca noticed Fuzz Wart was lying near one of the huge pillows on the bed. "Okay, who is this guy carved out of cream cheese and why haven't I heard about him before?" Sandy lit up a cigarette.

"No one special...and when did you begin smoking in your house?"

Sandy, taking a long drag, answered, "I smoke where and when I want. So...tell all. Are you two dating? Here I thought you were lonely and needed a little push in the right direction for some male companionship and you show up with one of the Greek Gods."

"Oh, Sandy, quit being so dramatic. He's just my neighbor and nothing more. He's new to the area and I thought it would be good for him to meet people...that's all."

"Good...can I have him? Just kidding," Sandy laughed

"I really don't know much about him. I thought it would be nice to walk into a party with someone for a change."

"Hey, kiddo, it's *me* you're talking to. Lets go out there and have some fun..it's Sunday and tomorrow starts a whole new work week."

"For some," Rebecca whispered under her breath as she followed Sandy out to the living room where the party was well on the way.

"Hey, maybe I can get you on at the newspaper. What do you think?"

"As what? Delivery girl with her own bike?" Rebecca walked toward the kitchen.

"Quit being so damn negative! Lighten up, will you? Eric, see if you can cheer her up, because you look like the kind of guy who can do a lot of cheering. I need to mingle with the natives." Sandy smiled as she gave Rebecca a kiss on the cheek and winked at Eric.

"Meet anyone interesting yet?"

"Only you." Eric raised his glass for a toast.

"Want to step out for a little fresh air?" Rebecca was feeling flushed.

"Sure." He escorted her through the French doors to the patio.

The patio looked more like a solarium with all of Sandy's plants. Rebecca sat on the wooden bench looking out across the golf course.

"I've played this course."

"I've never played golf, though Robert played every Sunday." Rebecca frowned. "How old are you?"

"Thirty…I'll turn Thirty-one this November."

"And where do you work?"

"I'm the new station manager for WBGL Channel 8 TV."

"Where did you say you lived before?"

"California, L.A. to be exact." Eric continued, "It will be hard for me to get use to the change of seasons here."

"Especially this winter coming up. At least you have a couple of months before it gets really cold."

"Have you lived here all of your life?" Eric wanted to know more about this intriguing woman.

"Born and raised."

"Ever want to live somewhere else?"

"Not really, my family is here…and being near Columbus, there is so much to do."

"Hey…you guys alright out here?" Sandy asked while peeking through the door. "Get back in here and join the party."

The rest of the afternoon went by smoothly. Rebecca enjoyed talking to the guests and forgetting about her life for a while.

The guests began to leave so Rebecca and Eric decided it was time to go as well. She kissed Sandy on the cheek, "I'll call you tomorrow."

"We'll have lunch." Looking at Eric, she said, "Nice to meet you and hope to see more of you."

Eric and Rebecca were silent for most of the drive home. He seemed preoccupied.

They were nearing the apartment complex and she asked, "Did you have a good time today?"

"Yes, thank you for inviting me."

"You seem distracted …was anything wrong?"

"I was thinking of a way to ask you out to dinner tomorrow night…how do you think I should go about it?" Eric leaned over to her side of the car.

"Oh…I've got butterflies, Eric, like I'm in uncharted territory. I've only been with my husband."

"Don't you mean your *ex*-husband? And I'm only asking you to dinner, Rebecca, not to bed." Eric smiled.

"Okay," Rebecca agreed as she thought to herself; *a real date with a man…am I really ready for this?*

Chapter Four

As Rebecca walked into her apartment, Alix was hanging the phone up. "So…how was the brunch?"

"Nice. And my neighbor…Eric…went with me."

"What, the hot blond guy? When did you invite him?"

"It was a spur of the moment thing…he happened to be outside when I was getting ready to leave and I just blurted out if he wanted to come, and to my surprise he did." Rebecca smiled

"Mom…you never do anything spur of the moment."

"I know. There are a lot of things I haven't done before, but I have a feeling that is about to change."

"Okay, well, I'm packed up, but I used all of the Tide…sorry, mom."

Rebecca helped Alix carry her bags out to the car.

"Mom…Earth to Mother…H-e-l-l-o!"

Rebecca recovered, "What were you saying?"

"I said…I used all of your Tide…and when is a good time to bring Scott by for dinner this week?"

"Any day."

"Tuesday night okay?

"Sure."

"Okay, then." Alix kissed her mother on the cheek.

Rebecca watched her drive off. As she walked into the apartment, she felt that empty feeling again. Walking over to where she had laid the Sunday paper on the coffee table, she didn't have the energy to look at the classified ads. She decided to call it a night and curl up with a good book. After all, tomorrow was another day.

Chapter Five

Hearing her alarm buzzing, Rebecca stirred in bed. Blinking her eyes, she focused on the light streaming in her window. She decided to get up, shower, dress and start the day. As she was about to put on her jacket, the doorbell rang. She was greeted by Eric, standing at her door with a smile across his face.

"Good morning, lady…today is your lucky day." He boasted.

"Oh?"

"Yes. You're coming with me to the station." Eric didn't seem like a man that would take no for an answer.

"Why?"

"Because I'm hiring you as my assistant." Eric continued, "You are just what I'm looking for, the job pays well, and offers great benefits—besides working for me, that is." Eric began walking to the car.

"Wait a minute…I don't know the first thing about working in a television station. Why would you want to hire me?"

Eric turned to face her. "You said you needed a job. I need an assistant. I feel that you're perfect because you are intelligent, classy, and I like you. As far as not knowing about television, you'll learn. Are you coming or not?"

Rebecca rolled her eyes, then smiling, she tilted her head asking, "Do you have a dental plan?"

Eric smiled as he opened the car door for her. "Besides, we can car pool."

He pressed his hand on the small of her back and Rebecca knew that what she felt was a future offering happiness and respect.

About the author:

Words run through my veins like paint onto an artist canvas. My mother is convinced I inherited the love for words from her first cousin Robert E. Lee the playwright. He was famous for such works as "Inherit the Wind," "Auntie Mame" and many other screenplays that he had co-created with his partner Jerome Lawrence. I am a 43 year old "domestic engineer"—at least that title is allotted to me when we fill out our taxes each year. In retrospect, this means a wife and mother of two daughters and five cats. Our eldest daughter, Jessica, is a freshman in college and I home school our eight year old, Alixandra. I was born in Ohio, moved to Florida after college where I pursued my career in social work. After eight years in Florida, my husband was transferred to South Carolina where I had an opportunity of being a Social Service Director for a Rehabilitation Center. By my late thirties I felt something was missing, so I tried my hand at painting, using oils as my medium. Though painting was fun, it still didn't quite hit the mark. When Alix was almost a year old, my husband was transferred to Pennsylvania, and by this time I had spent the majority of my life living in the South. People in Pennsylvania were different and didn't appreciate my expansive personality. At this time, my husband, Richard, and I decided that I should stay home with the girls to help adjust to the move and such. After knitting about a thousand wash cloths, baking several dozen loafs of bread, trying my hand at the culinary arts, painting and reading books, I started writing. I had written an article about one of our cats and *Cat Fancy* published that work in 2005. I have even been published on About.com with a couple articles about the history of the area we live in. I began writing all of the time, creating characters that were alive and real to me. Scribes Valley Publishing was the first contest I have ever entered. Last year my stories didn't make the cut; however, the constructive criticism that the Editor at Scribes Valley Publishing gave me was priceless. I value their U-Write It Challenge each week; this tool has helped me mature into a better writer. I have been seriously writing for seven years. This is my own philosophy: everyone has a thought, everyone has a feeling, everyone has a voice, everyone has something to say and to me writing is the gift.

HAUNTED HOUSES
©2007 by Chrissy K. McVay

My cajun cousin dances naked with ghosts in his haunted house. I visualize his bare, black skin sparkling in the moonlight with muscles twitching like the tail of a Siamese cat. Cooley found a broken down California house he could buy cheap after the previous owners died and left their spirits behind. My cousin jokes that the former owners had no idea how already crowded with spooks this house was or they would've tried to die somewhere else.

Cousin Cooley says he looks at the ocean for hours each night. "A trail of poetry seeps onto my pages as if hoodoo has taken me over," he tells me.

"You mustn't channel with old ghosts," I warn. "They can get inside you."

"One can smile more through words than with their lips, and your words are frowning," Cooley whispers in his melodic voice that tingles through my brain.

"We're not a smiling bloodline," I say.

"You can always smile here, Philoma. No one will scold or tell you to behave. No one in this city behaves after dark. Come to the coast and leave them muck-boos behind. You've got the ugly spirit of that old Creole ghost of General Beauregard to tangle with back there. Nothing but the ghosts of dead gold seekers 'round here, and they're pretty nice fellas."

It's not the first time my cousin has begged. I want to go to California, but I know what can happen. "I've a readable face, Cooley. It'll betray me, and betray us!"

"And they'll do what? Hang us?" He laughs aloud. "No one comes here. They know this house jus' full of the dead. They're not certain I'm alive, either. The neighbors think the flash of my camera at night is restless auras of spooks bouncin' off the rotted roof beams."

I can hear it in his voice; he wants me there so bad it makes his heart ache, but this longing only causes me anger. Circumstances weigh heavy on my heart. "It's impossible," I say.

Each member in the Boudreaudine family has a chink in their mental faculties. Physically, most of our brood is sound and lives nearly to one-hundred years old. This is a sad thing, because by the twilight of our lives, we've usually done something hideous to break our own hearts and spirits.

My mother has an odd ticking in her brain that causes her to get very upset over missing socks. She believes it's a terrible omen and she must find them before a bad thing happens. With her father, it was the passing hour of twilight to darkness that caused him anxiety. He never missed a sunset and refused to come inside until he'd watched the orange glow sink below the mucky waters of Cane's Bayou behind our house. I blame the mental chinks for the problem between me and Cooley.

I first noticed we were in trouble when I was thirteen and he turned fourteen. We lived four houses away from one another. I feared our secret would show on my face.

"Da Boudreaudine's gotta piss-poor poker face," my grandmother used to tease. My expressions have always been the cause of my own betrayals. Now it prevents me from being with Cooley.

I don't mind the idea of ghosts. Spirits and voodoo have always been a part of our families' religion. Some say we can trace strains of my mother's blood back to Marie Laveau, the Voodoo Queen of New Orleans.

Even so, the fact that I've murdered someone chills me. I don't wish to meet my victim's spirit in a dark corner of Cooley's haunted California house, and the soul I killed has good reason to want to find me.

"Ghosts aren't cruel," Cooley assures me. "Living people are the creatures you have to watch out for."

"Don't I know that," I agree. People sense the 'strangeness' in our blood. Whites in particular do their best not to talk to us. A white girl in the second grade once told me that my black eyes haunted her in her dreams, like the eyes of an angry crow.

"Anastacia won't know what you did," Cooley says. Even several years after her death, he's careful what is said over the phone or in our e-mails.

"Stacia locked eyes with me," I argue. "Toward the end, when her head turned slightly. She sucked in some of my spirit in her last moments of living."

I can't help but blame Stacia for her premature death. She won't think it's her fault, though, and the *Lwa* are powerful supernatural spirits when hungry for revenge. If they can take control of you during their journey from life to death, there's little you can do to shake 'em off.

Stacia had always wanted Cooley. She once begged me to use my knowledge of Vodun to make him fall in love with her. But I knew the real reason Cooley never looked at Stacia in that way. All the other boys couldn't help but stare into Stacia's flawless face and fall deeply in love.

I pretended to make a strong *gris-gris* for her. I'd soak ginger root in sweet oil or give her baking soda in a small sachet, telling her it was powdered cat's eyes. I knew the true magic she needed, but this was one thing I refused to help her with.

"I'll mail you something," Cooley promises, his words extremely breathy over the phone. "I've got to go now. Gotta photo shoot this evening for some rich lady's dog. She throws the thing a birthday party every year, and the money—it's very good. Ah, Philoma, you should see the outfits they put on their fancy doggies. There's one lady always dressin' her Jack Russell Terrier in a Zorro outfit," he laughs.

I sit down an hour later to leave Cooley an e-mail. *Ghosts want answers from the living,* I type slowly, pausing before I hit send. I'd never been a mean girl before I killed my best friend, nor after. It was just for that brief moment.

When the police wrested Stacia's limp body out after trawling St. John's Bayou, they were prompt to rule her drowning accidental. The gold plated hair barrette lay to one side of the bridge's paved edge…right where I said she'd reached over for it.

"A gift from her grandfather," her father explained, weeping as the officer bagged the barrette. "A trinket her grandfather would've fussed about if she went to his house without it in her hair!"

The father's tone was bitter and accusing. I remembered then how Stacia had said her father and the Grandfather always competed for her attention. She enjoyed being tugged on like a doll and received more expensive gifts than any girl I knew. "The spoils of Grandpa's war with Daddy," Stacia had told me.

I'd been the only one that heard the exact words Stacia spoke when her fingers accidentally flipped the expensive barrette from her hair. "Grandfather's paying my way through modeling school," she'd whined. "I can't just leave his gift there. He'll think I didn't like it. Hold my feet, Philoma. I know I can reach it."

I didn't think of anything cruel until Stacia's hand nearly closed over the barrette. She wouldn't have noticed my murderess expression at first. I wish I hadn't had a reason to kill her! Many times I could've used my talent as a Voodooienne to invoke the great Vodu to cause her harm, but the urge hadn't come to me before that day on the bridge.

I was grateful for all the tears I was able to coax from my eyes at the police station. If Cooley would've been there he'd known I was telling them lies. I hid my face in my hands just in case. Cooley figured out long ago how my lips quivered over my upper teeth when I was lying. The police just thought I was real upset after losing my friend.

Friday morning, I get a letter from Cooley. I finger his true birth name at the bottom: *Jacques Boudreaudine*. No one says our true names aloud, not even family members, though most are Catholic and claim to ignore superstitions. They know that people gifted in voodoo have real power to strike a person down if they know your real name. I'm so afraid the spirit of Stacia will find out my own true birth name: Adalenia.

A small piece of paper is hidden at the bottom of the envelope Cooley has sent me. He tries to conceal personal notes just in case my mother opens my mail. All of our family is snoopish. Cooley has included a poem titled 'Whisper'. I notice the paper is dabbed with cologne:

Whisper

Out of the heart of the night
Not infernal nor divine
Timeless and hidden from sight
From the night's heart into mine
Breathes a wandering spirit
Listen and you may hear it

This is what it sings to me:
I will love before I die
That tender intimacy
Which I thought had passed me by
Tonight is looking for me
I thought I had lost my mind
Along with my hope alone
Flying solo flying blind
But my address was unknown

Not in heaven nor in hell
But right here inside my heart
Love will find me wise and well
I can feel the magic start

Whisper you will come to me
Come and keep me company *

My toes tingle and I feel dizzy. Is he trying to hint to me that Stacia is there with him? I'm grateful my bedroom phone is at the far end of our house, overlooking the Cane Bayou where the peeper frogs and birds will drown out voices. When Cooley answers I'm suddenly unsure of what to say.

"Don't you dance naked with her ghost!" I shout. "Even if she *is* just a spirit, you'd be cheating on me. Stacia only wants you because you didn't never want her."

He pauses, and then is consumed with a fit of laugher. The jealousy in my voice gives him hope. "Are you coming to California? I need a Voodooienne to protect me from Anastacia."

It's my turn to pause. "I will," I said. "First I want to make a different *gri-gris*. Something stronger, in case she finds me."

"Do you remember Aunt Saloppe's pool?" he asks.

I blush as I recall our first French kiss. One hand brushes my hardening nipples. I can almost feel his fingers on my face again. I remember him naked at that early age, his skin shined up with droplets of chlorine water. We'd been playing Marco Polo in the above ground pool with a high bamboo fence all around. When I'd come up from under the water, I didn't realize my bikini top had dropped off. My breasts were barely developed, though I was almost fourteen. I was so embarrassed. But the intense gaze of longing in Cooley's eyes made me slow to cover myself. Instead, I lowered my arms, suddenly wanting him to see me nude. The wetness between my legs was thicker than the water and my heart trumpeted like Romans were charging.

"One is larger than the other," he'd said softly.

The hurt showed in my face. "They didn't start growing at the same time," I stuttered. "Screw you!" I'd screamed, humiliated. I pitched forward and shoved him under the water.

He came up coughing. "No, Philoma…their differentness makes them perfect," he said seriously. "Don't you see?" He'd closed the gap between us and kissed me long. I'd had 'pecks' on the lips and cheeks from boys, but this was different. His mouth was quickly over my nipples, the kisses tender because he realized my new breasts might be sore. We touched each other all over, trembling and seeking. His penis felt like velvet in my hands, blossoming between my palms. We groped until we heard Aunt Saloppe calling us in for lunch.

Later, when my breasts caught up to one another I felt they'd lost some of their splendor. I mourned when I gazed at them in front of a mirror. They were too perfect, like Stacia's. Cooley often said Stacia's plastic 'Barbie-body' truly bored him. He could look at her naked and fall right to sleep, he'd joke.

"Philoma, are you still there?"

I release a whimsical sigh. "I love you. I don't care who might be listening."

"Did you get the poem?"

"Yes. I thought it was about her, but you'd been thinking of me?"

"I'll send you money for a plane ticket." His voice is the most cheerful I've ever heard it.

"I'll pack," I promise. I burn two blue candles for love and luck before I shove my clothes into travel bags. I can't help thinking about Stacia again. It might not be so bad to see her spirit. Sometimes I think I need to tell her what she did wrong.

We were walking on the bridge and were so peaceful until she told me, "I'm going to 'out' your cousin Cooley."

I remembered how she had that determined look, the one that usually got us both into trouble. "What do you mean?" I felt the blood drain from my face, but she didn't even notice.

"I know why he doesn't try to kiss me or even talk to me like most boys do," Stacia said. "Cooley is Gay. It would be better if his mother knew he was homosexual so she could help him adjust. Don't you see how he struggles with his secret?" She'd pulled her lovely piano playing fingers through her curls.

How I envied those black curls that flounced across her shoulders. She was flawless physically, but her mind could be wicked and her words often hurt people. I couldn't tell her the real secret Cooley struggled with, and telling Aunt Manbo her only son was homosexual would've likely killed the woman. It was bad enough that her husband had run off with a younger woman right before Cooley was born. Manbo could endure no more heartache. Being a devout Catholic, Aunt Manbo would think a gay son was another tragedy in her life.

"You should leave him alone," I said.

Stacia just rolled her beautiful, dark eyes. She was a stirred up busy-body to the bone and had nothing better to do. It was then that her fingers caught on her barrette and flung it to the side of the bridge. We both ran to peer over and saw it on the ledge. Then the evil thought came.

"Can you hold my legs for me, Philoma?"

I hear that question over and over in my head now. How I wish I'd told her to forget about the silly piece of jewelry, even if it *was* made out of gold.

***

Cooley meets me at the airport and we kiss like we're any other couple in love. No one knows us. No one will care. I thought I'd miss the earth smell of the swampy Louisiana Bayous, but I don't. The fear of someone reading the truth in my face has left me. I'm not being watched. Perhaps Stacia's spirit was in the swamps after all, or the bank of St. John's Bayou, skimming along in the silty mud.

I can't see the spirits at first when I enter the California house. They are shy and peaceful ghosts. I dance naked with Cooley in his haunted rooms while the candlelight brushes our shadows like a hand tenderly buttering the softest bread ever baked. We can finally hold back no longer and make love with the moon shining through a bedroom skylight, pressing hard so our souls might crash into each other if we died at the same time.

I've found the strength to let go of all our shame in these rooms. I can forget we're not supposed to open our bodies to one another according to somebody's law in a book I've never seen. It's not until the next morning that I realize something in me has shifted into some dark place. My face appears to be the same as I gaze in the mirror, but somehow it isn't me at all. Then I smell a familiar scent. It's the lemon fresh odor of one of Stacia's expensive perfumes.

I tie a bright Tignon around my hair and prepare to light three white candles; one for each year Stacia has been dead. "How wise of you, Stacia," I laugh. "You knew I'd lead you to him eventually." I sigh and prepare a cup of blackberry tea. "Gal, this is gonna be a long battle between the two of us…"

*Whisper, *a poem by Steven Curtis Lance (copyright 2006), is used in this short story with the author's written permission.*

About the author:

Chrissy K. McVay's short stories have appeared in *Wild Violet Magazine*, *Foliate Oak*, *Aim* and various other publications. Her first novel, *Souls of the North Wind* was published June 2005 and was a Silver winner of the 2005 *ForeWord Magazine*'s Book of the Year Contest. Her essay "Soul-Saver Horse" was included in the anthology: *Angel Horses; Divine Messengers of Hope*. Chrissy is currently working on a second novel while enjoying life in the mountains of Western North Carolina with her family (which includes two Golden Retrievers). You can view an extended profile and other posted short stories and poems at: authorsden.com/chrissykmcvay.

CASEY'S CASKET
©2007 by Mike Tuohy

Casey regarded my draft card as he might a Valentine from a fat girl. "Selective Service, huh? Makes you feel really special, don't it?" He handed it back and plucked the smoldering joint from my fingers.

One of the late-running school busses finished discharging its unruly load and pulled out, bathing us in blue-tinted exhaust. Having just vented a long-held lungful of smoke, I hoped the hydrocarbon-laden air would somehow enhance my buzz. "If I'm lucky, which I doubt, they will be very selective. Do I look a little bow-legged to you?"

Casey strained to hold in his last toke as he spoke. "Why don't you ask Rhonda? She's always checking you out."

That pained me because I knew it wasn't true. Still, something that resembled Rhonda grew large in his mirrored sunglasses. It was a funhouse image of a tall, dark-haired ectomorph. I turned to give her a profile that shielded the zit on the left side of my nose.

In actuality, Rhonda was only a little above normal height for a girl, but she had the gaunt aspect of an underground comic speed freak. In her biker boots, black hip-huggers, knit rainbow shirt and headband, she projected biker-Indian-warrior-princess. "So, Wooten, you going to burn that draft card or are you a tool of the running yellow imperialist dogs?"

She had the Commie patter down, but the fact that she was talking to me was all the convincing I needed. I would have set my hair on fire if I thought it would impress Rhonda. I pulled out my wallet.

Casey seized my wrist. "That's not how you do it, man. Simply burning paper is not the point. It has to be part of a public demonstration."

Rhonda nodded at his wise words. She had pursued Casey since our freshman year. When he was dropped from the basketball team for his long hair, she quit the drill team. When he ran for student council on the Revolution Party ticket, she made outrageous posters for his campaign. When his letter decrying the dress codes that had gotten him suspended was published in Atlanta's notorious underground paper, the *Great Speckled Bird*, she started hawking copies on campus, getting herself ejected from school for a week.

Rhonda ground a half-smoked Virginia Slim into the sand of the student smoking area's official ashtray. She was the only one who seemed to use it. "You know, I'm putting together a march against the war on May Day. That would be a perfect time to make a statement."

Casey looked decidedly disinterested. "Good luck with that. I have other plans."

"On May Day? What's happened to you, man? It's like you just don't care anymore."

He regarded his filterless Camel as if it were a gem. "I really don't think getting our friend Wooten in trouble with the Federal Government is much of a bold action on your part."

"Hey, jerk! I burned my bra last year and I got suspended for three days. I'd do it again!"

Casey grinned in the way that nearly always presaged something unkind. "Rhonda, you burning your bra is about as much a sacrifice as Principal Pugh shaving his head."

By her expression, it was clearly not necessary to point out that male pattern baldness had completely run its course on Mr. Pugh's scalp. I would never understand why Casey treated her this way. Even on the verge of tears, she still looked incredibly hot. Most of her epithets were drowned out by the first period bell but I thought I heard the words 'counter-revolutionary' and 'motherfucker' as I followed Casey up the echoing stairwell.

During the eighty or so seconds it took us to get to Mrs. Saxon's Modern English Literature class, I sorted out what I had learned. For one thing, Casey was a tit man. So was I, but small breasts were not a deal-breaker. Secondly, Casey had a real mean streak in him. I might have to distance myself from him for awhile if I was going to make a play for Rhonda. The fact that she was really mad at him might make this plan work.

As soon as we settled at our desks in the back row, Casey slowly exhaled the two lungs worth of smoke he had taken in at the bell. With parental permission, smoking was allowed at our school in the designated area we had just left. Casey just seemed to feel a need to push the limits.

Mrs. Saxon, our English Literature teacher, had just stepped to the blackboard with a legal pad ominously covered with her tiny scrawl and began to transcribe. I knew we would have some time to kill. "So, Casey, how'd it go with the counselor yesterday?"

The last wisps of blue-gray smoke were just leaving his nostrils. He took in several deep breaths before answering. "He wanted to know if I ever considered suicide while I was in woodshop."

I considered for a moment how I would have answered such a question. Ending my life was not something I had ever seriously considered except as a fleeting thought when a girl made it clear she was not interested in me—or guys like me. There was some flimsy logic to denying her a chance to reconsider that soon passed into plain old anger, misogyny, and self-pity. It was hard to imagine that Casey ever had to go through this. Rhonda was not the only fine woman he had spurned.

I knew better than to ask his reasons. I confined my inquiries to the mundane struggles against the system and the Man. "So, what did you tell him?"

"I said, 'Yeah, man, but I really want to die in English Lit.'"

We shared a snuffling doper laugh, drawing a brief glare from Mrs. Saxon. She went back to eviscerating *Catcher in the Rye*, ruining it for us all.

"Bet that freaked him out," I said quietly. I really needed to pass this class and my only hope for that was good conduct. Casey went on in his cafeteria voice.

"Yeah, he's got his fucking psychology degree hanging on the wall. He's heard it all. He gave me back my plan and told me to talk to my clergyman. I didn't have the heart to tell him I'm a fucking atheist."

Mrs. Saxon's chalk squeaked at the vulgarity but she soon recovered and went on writing. She had sent Casey to the office too many times for this infraction without effect. Odds were that she was going to just give him a D for the quarter and pass him on to the next teacher. I hoped she would do the same for me. "So, why did you have to go?"

"Mr. Wise turned my woodshop project down. I guess it made him uncomfortable, what with his upcoming operation and all." He unrolled a piece of graph paper half-again the size of my desktop. The plan was a thing of beauty, drafted in black ink and neatly hand-lettered in block print. Casey liked to say he had enrolled in woodshop to 'dodge drafting'. In truth, he was already a master draftsman and artist.

I had assumed that, like me, he wanted to make hash pipes, stash boxes or maybe even an elaborate hookah. This plan of his went far beyond that. Casey was thinking long-term. He wanted to build a casket.

I was not as surprised at his choice as I was at the magnitude of the undertaking, if it could be called that. "Twenty board-feet of black walnut? What did that cost?"

"Two-hundred bucks, give or take."

"Jesus! Where do you get that kind of money?"

For once, Casey took his voice down to a barely audible level. "You remember that half-pound of Mexican weed I brought back from Texas?"

"Yeah. Got any more?"

"Sold out last week."

Thanks to actions by President Nixon, it was a sellers' market for pot in Georgia. By the peculiar math of the high school drug trade, I figured that half-pound had expanded to a good twelve ounces. At twenty dollars a bag, he could buy the wood, the brass hardware and line the box with velvet.

I wondered how the assistant woodshop teacher would regard Casey's project. Mr. Norman would be in charge while Mr. Wise was hospitalized for a gall bladder operation. "Have you shown Norman your plan yet?"

"I saw the note Mr. Wise left for him. It just said I would have to resubmit my term project. He'll probably reject it, too."

"Tell him it's a speaker cabinet. Add some dadoes and dovetail joints. Mr. Norman loves that kind of shit."

Casey snatched the plan from my desk. "Does this look like a speaker cabinet to you?" He sounded pissed.

"Does if you lose the handles and hinges."

"What about the lid? He's going to expect big round holes."

"So, you make a front piece out of cheap wood. A decoy. The lid's the same dimensions as the back, just make two. You can seal and finish one at home if you have to."

Casey had a way of baring his front teeth like a woodchuck when in deep thought. It was the goofy flaw in his otherwise perfect façade of coolness, one I dared not point out. He had one last comment as Mrs. Saxon turned to face us. "Wooten, you may have more wisdom than your grade point average would suggest."

A week later in woodshop, I came across Casey as he arranged three speakers (tweeter, mid-range and woofer) on a sheet of high-quality veneer. Once centered and spaced to his liking, he outlined them in pencil and marked the screw holes with care.

"Damn, Casey! You could have used particle board."

"I could have, but I wanted Mr. Norman to know I was serious about my intentions. Besides, I need something to do between now and when the truck gets here."

"What truck?"

"The one bringing the walnut. It had to be special ordered from Ohio. It's running late."

That explained why Mr. Norman had paced the loading dock throughout the first half of class. He ducked out several times to venture into the parking lot.

Principal Pugh came by and was clearly disturbed to find a roomful of teenagers operating lathes, saws and routers without adult supervision. I tilted my lamp base up to hide the internal tubing that had no place in an illumination device. He eyed my work area suspiciously. "Mr. Wooten! Do you know where your teacher is?"

Fortunately, Mr. Norman soon arrived, out of breath but not words. "Principal Pugh! You're just in time! The truck is on its way!"

"Mr. Norman! You shouldn't leave these students unattended."

"I'm real sorry about that. I just stepped out for a minute. It's not every day that anybody goes over their allotment. Casey went way over and I would hate to disappoint him. Have a look at the plan he drew up."

The County school system provided each student with nine dollars and seventy-five cents for materials. That was usually enough to buy pine for a small bookcase or mahogany for a gun rack. Black walnut was another matter. It was a wood so precious that its use was usually board or a moderate-sized plaque once the wood was cut, trimmed and planed.

Mr. Pugh eyed the drawing with a sour expression. He was a deeply religious man with no trust of teenagers, especially hippies. He turned it sideways, held it at arm's length and finally seemed satisfied that it would not accommodate a pair of students bent on fornication or escape. "Well, I suppose it is a worthy use of school materials and facilities."

"Oh, it's far more than that, Mr. Pugh. This is a sure-fire winner at the County Industrial Arts Fair."

The two men jutted out their lower lips like catfish and nodded at the plan in unison. I couldn't wait to tell Casey, but he was out in the parking lot, awaiting the truck.

Mr. Norman was the kind of guy who got a touch-up once a month. In between, he just kept his black hair slicked back with Vitalis. Even in Georgia, his Alabama heritage stood out. In a North Atlanta white suburban high school half-full of Yankee transplants, he was an anomaly. Not one to hide his real self or feelings, he rubbed his hands together as the truck backed in, making a little hop as the rear bumper contacted the dock pads with a *thud*. "Alright, y'all! Shut down your work stations and come on over to the loading dock. We have something special today."

Mr. Norman counted heads before flipping the switch that turned off the sawdust recovery and exhaust systems. Pulleys rumbled and the whining fans descended in pitch as if to let us know that we were about to experience something big. There was only so long a roomful of teenage boys would let the quiet prevail.

Mr. Norman raised his hand for silence. "Y'all listen up! Much as I hope some of you boys pursue a career in the industrial arts, I doubt you will get to see something like this very often. So, behold!"

He threw the latch and the rear door of the truck rolled up. The varied scents of exotic and ordinary woods washed over us. It was intriguing, even to the novice nose. Mr. Norman cradled the end of a plank and breathed in like an oenophile. "This here is black walnut, one of our finest domestically produced woods. Casey has put up two hundred of his own money that I know he worked hard for, but we're all going to learn a little bit about it, if that's alright with him."

Casey gave a slight nod. Mr. Norman launched into a rambling lecture as he inspected each rough-cut plank of the prized wood, making certain that each of us got a good look. He practically did a quarter of Casey's work, running each board through the planer just to see the lumber reveal its grain in all its glory. He even scooped a portion of the sawdust into a Mason jar to share with Mr. Wise at the hospital.

We didn't see Casey much at the smoking area over the next three weeks. He spent a lot of time after school in the woodshop. Mr. Norman was wrapped up in the project. I was there when Casey proposed using dovetail joints at the ends of the side panels. I thought Mr. Norman was going to cry.

Less than a week before the big May Day protest against the war in Vietnam, Casey surprised us with a visit. I was discussing a banner design with Rhonda as we shared a small joint. I had made a little progress with her. She actually sought me out at smoke time. If this bothered Casey, he didn't show it. He pulled out a cigarette and leaned against a pilaster, facing us without comment.

I held out my lighter. "Good to see you back with the living!"

Rhonda was less upbeat. "Yeah, Casey. We thought you and Mr. Norman were building a tree house together."

He regarded her with the same inscrutable stare he gave everyone, nodding slightly. "I have to wait a few days for the polyurethane to cure."

I took the opportunity to enlighten Rhonda about what a creepy guy Casey really was. I figured he wouldn't mind. "Believe it or not, Casey has constructed the most amazing casket to ever come out of the Conroy High School industrial arts program."

Rhonda's eyes widened. "You're building a coffin?"

Casey lit another cigarette from the one he had going. He had some catching up to do. I decided to answer on his behalf. "Solid black walnut, brass hardware, and purple velvet lining."

Rhonda handed me the roach we had been sharing and stepped right in front of Casey. "Can we use it in the peace march next week? It would be so perfect."

I was losing her.

Casey took half of his cigarette in a single drag and held it in awhile. "No," he said, exhaling. "I'll be needing it."

Rhonda turned to me. "Can you believe this asshole?"

It was an uncomfortable position for me, but if I was going to have to choose, I would go with her. "I could probably put one together. I'll have to make it out of plywood but we can paint it black."

Casey seemed to take offense at this idea. "That would be an abomination!" He paced a minute and threw his half-smoked Camel away, lit another and turned to Rhonda. "Tell you what, you can use my coffin, under one condition."

"Really?" She moved in close to him. Their cigarettes almost touched.

"Sure, you just have to carry it with me inside."

Rhonda looked at me as if I had just been drafted or at least promoted to the status of 'useful idiot'. "Deal!"

* * *

I met Casey at six a.m. at the woodshop loading dock with my Mom's station wagon, a baby blue 1962 Belair. It was a most unlikely hearse. As instructed, I brought sheets and blankets to protect the finish on his creation.

Mr. Norman had loaned Casey the back door key so he could work on his project after school. The janitor was used to seeing him around at odd hours so, instead of busting us for unauthorized entry, the man actually helped us load the casket into the car. It was a good thing. It weighed at least three-hundred pounds.

We had to fold the seats and leave the tailgate down to accommodate the length. Having no good way to tie it, Casey knelt on the front seat and held on to the rails he had installed that morning. It was clearly no speaker cabinet.

The student parking area was completely empty and I was able to park in the corner that was shaded by trees, the rear end facing into the bushes. We had to be careful. Principal Pugh, was expecting some sort of demonstration. Rhonda had distributed a mimeographed handbill replete with plagiarized revolutionary graphics picturing Asian peasants bearing pitchforks and automatic rifles. It called for all those who opposed the war to gather at the smoking area for an early morning rally.

This was a diversion. The real demonstration would start simultaneously at the opposite end of the parking lot. By the time Pugh realized that an honest-to-God coffin was heading up the sidewalk to his office, it would be too late. The whole world would be watching.

At least, that was the plan. As far as I was concerned, it was over before it started. The only volunteers I could find on such short notice were non-athletic potheads just like me. Worse than that, their heights varied from under five feet to over six. We were struggling along with baby steps as the side rails tried to pull our arms out at the shoulder sockets when Rhonda showed up with the bullhorn. "You need to carry him on your shoulders, people. We're making a statement here!"

One of the pallbearers, a rotund former chess-club champ named Gregg who preferred to be called 'Frodo', eyed me with sweaty anger. "Did she say 'him'? Is there somebody in this thing?"

I might not lie for the Revolution, but I would for Rhonda. "It's an effigy of Nixon. We're going to burn it."

Gregg/Frodo mulled it over and finally nodded approval. "Cool. Let's move." With that, he started to hoist the left rear corner.

Unfortunately, the rest of the contingent was not quite ready. The casket began to cant dangerously to the starboard. I rushed to the right front corner and tried to serve as a human jack. Instead, the box continued its forward and downward motion, striking my head and briefly rendering me unconscious. My last vision of the march was the sight of Casey rolling out on the pavement as a rainbow of pills erupted from his mouth.

***

The only record that survived was a wavy black and white video taken from the second story of the building by Roy Crump, president of the audio-visual club. Roy was a self-styled conservative who vocally supported Nixon and the war as a means of getting attention when surrounded by the freaks who gravitated to the audio-visual club. I figured he had only taped the proceedings because of a sick fascination with Rhonda. When he offered to give her a 'private screening' in the library after school, she asked me to come along.

Roy's broad face communicated his supreme displeasure at my presence. "So good to see you, Rhonda." There followed a long pause. "Wooten, I wouldn't think you'd really want to see this. Your performance is not exactly pleasant to watch."

I took the hint as a challenge. "What the hell! I've never been on TV before."

"It's just magnetic tape. It will be erased soon enough."

Rhonda gave me a grateful glance. "I don't have much time, Roy. Can we get on with it?"

He closed his eyes, perhaps savoring some unintended meaning from the phrase before he set about turning on the machine. "Certainly! Wooten, get the lights." A queasiness arose in my gut as he started to narrate. "OK, this is the part where Pugh confronts the chanting crowd at the smoking area."

It took a few seconds to get oriented. The players could be readily identified by hair. The freaks had plenty, the opposition, very little. The camera suddenly panned right.

"OK, this is where the coffin contingent reaches Pugh's office."

The image was broken into barely discernible ghosts cut by lines of gray. I could only tell which head was mine because I already knew the sequence of events.

"OK, here's where Casey starts freaking out."

I could almost feel the motion again as the pallbearers started to sway.

"OK, this is where they drop the casket."

The audio did not pick up the *thunk* of the wood against my skull against the decorative column nor the *crack* as it hit the pavement. My head began to throb as Roy went on.

"OK, this is where Casey rolls out!"

The fuzzy gray images did not do justice to the stew of multicolored pills that spilled from Casey's mouth. We skipped ahead to the arrival of the ambulance. Casey struggled only a little as the paramedics strapped him to the gurney. He didn't look quite so cool when they took off his sunglasses and pulled his puke-wet hair above the top of his scalp like an exclamation point. It was some time before one of the cops pointed to me. By then I was sitting up, rubbing my temples. I hoped nobody had recorded the interview in which they apparently determined that I was just naturally an idiot and therefore unworthy of prosecution.

Throughout the whole sad affair, a lone figure stood off to the side eyeing the coffin and sadly shaking his head. It took a second viewing before I recognized Mr. Norman.

Rhonda put her hand on Roy's hairy wrist. "Can we save this?"

"Afraid not. Coach Holland needs this reel for the next football practice and then the drama club wants to use it. Videotape is expensive."

The words of Gil Scott Herrin popped into my head. Unfortunately, they immediately dropped out of my mouth. "The revolution will not be televised."

Rhonda looked at me as one might a brain-damaged person, then her lips formed an exaggerated sneer. "Shut up, Wooten!"

I left Rhonda and her tiny jugs with Roy.

Casey wouldn't be coming back to Conroy High. I overheard the whole sad story during one of my mom's bridge club sessions. I hadn't known that he had killed his little brother when he was ten. It was an accident. They had taken his grandfather's tractor out at night. Casey barely survived the rollover himself. Apparently, he had not gotten over it—not that anybody ever could. He would spend the next few years at some sort of rehab center, safe from the draft and hopefully from himself.

Mr. Wise had died shortly after his surgery and Mr. Norman was promoted to head of the Industrial Arts Department. The class had been constrained from using power tools pending his return from the funeral and all seemed genuinely glad to see him back making his rounds. I was manually sanding my term project when he came to me. The way he held and looked at my bogus lamp base, it could have been a grenade, a baby doll or a bottle of liquor.

"Good to see you taking pride in what you do, son." His voice lacked the old boom and conviction. The words came out as if he was struggling with an unfamiliar hymn.

I looked at the hunk of wood that I had come to know so well over the preceding six weeks. Unadorned straight sides, angular and blocky, it would be a pretty bland hookah. With a little improvement, I thought, it might actually make a decent table lamp. "Mr. Norman, I'd like to take down some of these edges and give it a little class. Would you mind checking me out on the router?"

He looked at me as if he thought I might be conning him. I had never before shown any interest in exceeding the minimum effort required for a passing grade. "You serious, son?"

"It's going to be for my mom. She likes nice stuff."

That seemed to satisfy him. He cleared his throat and spoke in the manner of a shaman sharing a long held secret. "The router is what elevates wood projects from objects to heirlooms, even works of art. Of course, we're not just here to make pretty things, if you know what I mean, but beauty coupled with function can be the greatest testament to God's faith in Man."

I knew the mantra. "But function first."

He smiled as if hearing someone repeat his own words soothed his soul. "I'd be right proud to instruct you on the use of this fine tool."

As Mr. Norman demonstrated the subtleties of the various bits, it occurred to me that this man would not mind dying in woodshop, even if he was devoured by the planer or ripped up the middle by the table saw. In the meantime, it was his life.

Excelling at woodworking was hardly my long-term goal, but I supposed it wouldn't hurt to master something besides rolling a joint one-handed before I graduated high school.

"Make certain you have your board and guide bar firmly secured. Now, you sort of have to feel your way, depending on the material. You don't want to go too fast or too slow, you can actually burn the wood, and it's a bear to sand that out once it's cut. You know exactly what you want to do now?"

"Yes, sir!"

"Alright, then! Plan your work and work your plan." The voice was coming back. He even smiled as he handed me the router.

The determined whine of the motor and the scent of fresh-cut wood banished any doubts about the righteousness of my newfound cause. The Revolution would have to get by without me for awhile. It seemed I had enlisted myself as an apprentice woodworker.

About the author:

I was born in Montclair, New Jersey during the Eisenhower Regime, moved to Georgia in 1965 and have resided within and around Atlanta ever since. Graduating from Georgia State University in 1980 with a BS in Geology I somehow ended up in the environmental consulting racket. In the meantime, I helped raise two sons (neither of whom resemble me but I'm not complaining because they're really smart). Currently dealing with mid-life crisis by writing stories I have accumulated over the years and intended to self-publish as a collection titled "Chicken Soup for Dummies." On advice of counsel,

I have redirected my efforts toward getting published elsewhere so I don't spend the next ten years in court (can't stand wearing a tie).

Publications:

Tuohy, Mike "Too Much Experience" *Sea Oats Review, Vol. 3*, 2005, pp. 36-39.

Tuohy, Mike "Baby Peas and Sweet Potatoes;" *Spout Magazine, Vol. 31* (in press).

Tuohy, M.A. "Albert's Tobacco and Confectionary Shop," *Lunch Hour Stories* (in press).

THE GREAT ANIMAL KINGDOM
ACCORDING TO TOVA JARVIS
©2007 by Tova Jarvis

I have great respect for the animal kingdom. Unfortunately, nature doesn't seem to be as fond of me as I am of it. Like a lot of things in my life, I'm fairly suspicious that it is out to get me. It may have all started when I said, "Salad? No, thanks, I'll take the juicy burger instead." Other than having my share of delectable, mouth-watering meat, I believe myself to be fairly innocent of any serious offense against Mother Nature...and if I could afford it, I would get a hybrid car.

Obviously, good intentions mean nothing and the attacks began long before I was even of driving age. I say attack and I mean *attack*. I've been stung by bees, bitten by spiders, eaten alive by mosquitoes, stepped on by donkeys, and chased by bats. There have even been a few pranksters, like mice who spring out of the bags I'm opening, much in the same way those cloth snakes pop out of a can of nuts. I'm sure I would have suffered one or two minor heart attacks if I wasn't busy ricocheting around the room along with the mouse. I just don't understand it, because I have always been the type of person who wouldn't hurt a fly. Ripping the legs off that spider with my bare hands was an accident and, believe me, I paid dearly for it by having the heebie-jeebies for at least a week. But flies, I have never touched.

Coming back from my parents' home last month (San Francisco Bay Area to Los Angeles), I took my usual route, which is a 300-plus mile trek across the flat landscape of California farm country. This stretch of road is also known more commonly as Highway 5, but I like to think of it as the long, black eternal asphalt that stretches into a twilight zone abyss of hypnotic, mind-numbingly, boring scenery where time never moves forward and you eventually go crazy. Fortunately, I'm already there, but even though I'm immune, it can still get to me at times.

Anyways, as I'm driving down the road at ninety miles an hour, keeping an eye peeled for coppers, all of a sudden the area around me is filled with butterflies. Hundreds and hundreds of these tiny *kamikaze* butterflies fill the air. Now, the news may have mentioned something about these butterflies migrating, but I have no doubt they were trying to sabotage my car. If they couldn't drive my car off the road with the sheer force of hundreds of winged bodies bombarding it, they knew that at least with their butterfly guts all over the windshield, they could hamper my vision. I don't know what makes me more upset; the fact that they were attempting to kill me or they were messing up a week old carwash. I, personally, think this is a sign of the beginning of the apocalypse. Doesn't the Bible mention something about swarms of butterflies with wings of fire, devouring the Earth or something?

But then, I have to say that I've been emotionally damaged from another experience with a winged creature. In this case, it was a bird. On my parents' property there happens to be a very large palm tree, which seems to be home to a lot of creatures. I never knew what was living up there half the time, but then I never really paid attention.

One spring, a bluejay couple took up residency and it wasn't too long before they had a family. Coming home one day, I happen to notice that a baby bluejay, still shedding its baby soft feathers, laid innocently at the bottom of the tree, making soft peeping noises. I, concerned for its safety because of the population of rogue cats roaming the neighborhood, went to investigate its condition. I had no sooner come within a few feet of it when a loud, shrill screech pierced the air. My body tensed suddenly for I had a feeling I was in mortal danger and I turned my head just in time to see a flurry of blue and black feathers making a beeline straight for my head. I ducked-- just missing it-- but, in my action, I failed to see the other angry parent and was instantly hit. In attack mode, the bluejays swooped down, knocking me about in a fury.

As they took a slight break to, I can only guess, ready the torpedoes, I saw my chance. Disoriented and whimpering, I raced to the safety of the door, flung it open, dove inside. Thinking that was the end of it, and because I'm not always too bright, I then cracked open the door, peering out. It was quiet. Maybe a little too quiet except for the innocent little "peep, peep." I opened the door a little wider and then heard the "caw" of the bluejays. There they were, perched on the roof, facing the door, just waiting for me. I slammed it shut.

So the lesson here today is never get on the bad side of a bluejay. The only people qualified to handle this sort of thing are the heroes of Disney cartoons. Not only can they pick them up but also they can get them to sing or whistle along with a song. For the rest of us, they're like the Italian mob of the bird family. They never forget and they strike their revenge with a vengeance, asking questions later. Those bluejays waited outside my front door for at least a month. I suddenly found myself getting into the habit of cracking open the door, bolting out, ducking, rolling, diving into bushes, and waving my arms wildly until I could get into the car. After awhile, I didn't even think that much about the routine till a neighbor asked me how that new medication was working out.

I like to believe the creators of "creature features" have it right. It doesn't matter if it's a giant snake, killer shark, bluejays or butterflies, nature refuses to be tamed and if it's willing to take you out without a moment's thought then why should you feel guilty about that juicy burger you really want to eat for lunch. Just make sure it's giant snake, killer shark, bluejay or butterfly burger. After all, what did a cow ever do to you?

About the author:

Tova graduated from San Francisco State with a degree in broadcasting but originally had aspirations of joining the circus as a lion tamer, a profession she would be perfectly suited for having worked at a law firm for the better part of five years. Sadly, though, she was afflicted with "freakyclownphobia"—the fear of freaky clowns and their phobias—and her dreams of circushood were permanently dashed. She settled for working at a visual effects studio in Los Angeles, spending her free time reading, writing, looking through thrift stores for treasures and just general procrastination. She loves nature, despite being convinced that it is out to get her, and daydreams of opening up her own hotdog stand. Feel free to drop her a note at tovajarvis@prodigy.net.

BUTTERFLIES GONE
©2007 by Patricia Dainty

It was the typical southern California summer night. Hot, with the smell of sweet orange blossoms in the air. The front door was open to allow the night breeze through. He showed up on the front porch, searching for my brother. Nervousness was the first emotion I felt. He asked for my brother, I replied, "He is not here." I slammed the door in his face, just as quickly as he had walked up. I had just turned eighteen, fresh on the euphoria of high school graduation 1969. Visions of attending college occupied my thoughts. Marriage after dating, all within the next six months was not in my plans.

He returned later in the week. Introductions and, oh yes! I had heard about him. He was the uncle of my best friend. To me, uncles were in their forties or fifties—not twenty-one, Marines, or handsome. He was a man, not like the boys I had been accustomed to dating. He was personable, smooth, and charming. I knew on our first date he was a flirt and skilled with the ladies, but that was, oddly enough, part of his appeal. There were signs of controlling behaviors and attitude I chose to ignore. The butterflies began that August day he first kissed me. By October we were engaged.

We underwent marriage counseling, a pre-requisite by the Methodist Church. The veins in his neck bulged with anger when the Rev. Miller suggested we were both too selfish to have our marriage last.

We began our journey of twenty-two years together February 1970.

Viet Nam took him away five weeks after we were married, and the fear of becoming a bride and a widow in the same year gripped my soul.

College, after the first semester was no longer a priority for me. Working part time at May's Department Store helped me pass time. When I was not working, Newport Beach became my refuge. I love the beach, the way the waves splash onto the sand, the gentle foam inching further and further up until it retreats back into the tide. Looking out to the horizon, I could imagine him at China Beach, DaNang, South Viet Nam. We were looking at the same sun, moon, and stars. This knowledge comforted me. Sitting on the beach surrounded by hundreds of people, I could become lost in his love letters which arrived regularly. I could cry and no one would notice.

The butterflies fluttered with each letter.

Butterflies were everywhere when I pulled up to Norton Air Force Base twelve months after he had left. Forgetting to put the car in gear, it came to a lunging stop. With the strains of the Carpenters' "We've Only Just Begun" blasting from the radio, I was out of the car and into his arms. The only fanfare the soldiers received that day was the screams of glee coming from their wives, girlfriends, and family.

We left California, making our home in a small rural town in Tennessee. The adjustment did not come easy for me. I was the typical beach girl, with the polka-a-dot bikini and hair that hung down my back.

The heat of that first summer was smothering. I was accustomed to heat but the humidity stifled every ounce of energy within me. To refresh myself, the country store down the road became an everyday occurrence. The old block building with a wood floor welcomed me with a familiarity which took me back in time to when my family would travel Highway 66 from California to Ralston, Oklahoma to visit my grandparents.

The country store was filled with odds and ends needed for country living: shovels, hoes, etc. Dill pickles were kept in a large wooden barrel, fresh for the taking. And then there was the deli counter! Rolls of fresh bologna, ham, roast beef, and cheeses of every variety. Pauline, the owner of the store, would cut half-inch slices of bologna off the roll, place them in wax paper, and then into a brown paper bag to keep them fresh until I walked back home.

The memory of that small country store makes me recall the times when the butterflies were fluttering and flying.

When the cool autumn air finally came to Tennessee, I relished the change in seasons. Driving in the country and watching the leaves turn to crimson and gold, we saw a barn smoking from its rafters. I was wondering why he wasn't concerned about the smoke when he explained, "That is tobacco curing. The farmers smoke the tobacco to cure it and then dry it to make it pliable to tie."

This was my introduction into the main source of income for many families in the area: raising tobacco. As an avid non-smoker it surprised me when the smell of the smoking tobacco mingling with the cool air gave me a sense of comfort.

Over the course of the next years, our lives became entwined with his admission into college, my work, and what little time we had together. We lived in married student housing for the three years it took him to graduate. The GI Bill, his part time job, and my jobs at the factory and the phone company got us through. Remembering back, we were broke! We married for love, certainly not money. But the cost of tuition, books, housing, food, and the never-ending list of incidentals was staggering.

With my first job, I stepped into a world which was completely foreign to me. I had never been inside a factory before, much less work in one. My air of nervousness brought unwanted attention to myself. Whispers of "Who is she?" "She doesn't belong here" followed me every day. Living on the Cumberland Plateau of Middle Tennessee, people appeared to be stuck in history long past. They reminded me of the Hatfields and the McCoys.

The factory was dirty, smelly, and hot, with no air conditioning. I was to cut leather into pieces to be assembled into boots. Terrified I would cut my hands on the electric saw, I was exceedingly slow. I never made my daily quota, and no quota meant only minimum wage. I was miserable, but bills needed to be paid.

I was finally moved into a department where I could actually make more than minimum wage. The job description was to put pairs of boots into a vise, tie them together, and, when a bundle was created, throw them into a bin.

I was making one hundred dollars a week; we could spend more than ten dollars a week on food! I cried when a gaunt looking woman came over to say, "Honey, I'm just going to have to bump you." I looked down at her diamond-crusted fingers wondering how much one of those rings had cost.

I quit. Thank goodness the phone company called!

He believed it was more important for him to graduate from college than me. Graduation rolled around in August 1974. I was so proud of him! I wouldn't have to worry about working any more. He would take care of me and the baby I was carrying.

The fall of 1974 brought the birth of our first child, a girl! We tried for two years to have a baby. Charting my temperature became a monthly habit, until finally the long anticipated miracle happened. Thinking to myself, *I will be responsible for another human being for life*, my hands trembled as I wrote the check out at the doctor's office. I knew our baby was wanted, longed for, and already so loved.

My pregnancy was uneventful; I didn't even experience morning sickness, just the joy of pregnancy! We arrived at the hospital around midnight on a cold, November night. We both were so excited and nervous about the delivery. In 1974 he couldn't be with me in the labor or delivery room. Lying in the labor room, I wished the nurses would allow him to come sit by me.

Labor was uneventful at this point so I went to sleep. Two hours later, the nurse requested I not chew on the gas mask! In between the space of reality and a drug-induced twilight sleep I remember screaming for him right before I was wheeled into delivery. Watching the mirror above me, I knew he was missing the most amazing event! She was beautiful, perfect, and ours!

As they rolled me out of delivery, he came up the corridor and ran circles around the gurney, beaming and asking, "Did you see her? Did you see her?"

Butterflies had never been so abundant!

We moved into our first house. I took great pleasure in making it our home. With the demands of a newborn, I scarcely realized he was gone more and more, until the night of our fourth wedding anniversary. I sat in the rocking chair he bought the same day we brought our new daughter home. She and I rocked into the wee hours of the morning. Where was he? This was our anniversary.

I watched until the headlights of his car finally appeared in the driveway. Laying her down softly in her crib, tears streamed down my face. With a look of defiance on his face, his answer was, "Out with my friends."

The butterflies weren't fluttering.

Work became his obsession. Climbing the ladder of success to General Manager of the local electrical cooperative was his goal, all for the betterment of the family; never mind the time it consumed or the changes which were occurring in him.

His new friends from work were younger than he and single. He was jealous of their freedom. They could spend their money any way they chose. He indulged in late night poker games with them, coming home with the smell of cigarettes and beer on his clothes.

He felt trapped in our marriage. Guilt would not allow him to leave. No one in his family had ever been divorced before, much less the youngest son and most adored of his fifteen siblings. The matriarchal figure of his family would be devastated. She loved me as a daughter, but he could not bring himself to tell her.

We rode the carousal we called our life. "Everything will be okay," he would say. I clung to these words knowing full well someday he would change his mind again. Derogatory remarks from him came more and more often. Coming from your soul mate, words sting harder than any slap of the hand. Physical abuse was never the problem. Emotionally, I had become his scapegoat.

One day, I could hear the closet door open and the angry tone under his mumbled breath. Rushing down the hallway to see what it was I had done this time, I could sense the tension in the air. Never before had I seen this look on his face. I watched him yank the shirts I had just ironed off the hangers, stomping them into the carpet.

The butterflies in my stomach were too afraid to flutter!

Brushing past me, he said, "You can't even iron right! You didn't put in enough starch!"

Waiting for him to leave, I silently wondered while picking up his shirts, *Why, if I can't iron them right, won't you let me take them to the cleaners?*

Intimidation is a powerful force!

***

Waves of morning sickness gave it away. I had not been sick with my first pregnancy. I so loved being pregnant the first time around. I knew he wasn't going to be pleased. I hesitated telling him.

"I'm not jumping up and down for joy," was his response.

I thought in time he would come around and join me in the thrill of another child. I was wrong!

Driving together to Nashville, he calmly stated, "I am leaving after the baby is born."

Panic filled me. I knew he wasn't happy, but we still had some happy times. I could not hold back the tears.

"You better not say anything to any of our friends, and stop the crying."

Angrily, I told him, "Why wait until the baby is born? You can leave now."

As it turned out, he didn't leave. Made no sense to me how he could justify leaving me with two babies, but not when I was pregnant. I was grateful he couldn't leave at all.

We built our second home in the country. He worked until dark and all day on the weekends. He worked himself to exhaustion. The house was built on the same road the majority of his family lived. Privacy was nonexistent. The house was small, adorable, and comfortable. We both were proud of our home.

I enjoyed being a stay-at-home mom. A career woman I was not! Figuring I had all the time in the world to work when our toddler grew up, I was disappointed when he suggested I go to work to help pay off the mortgage on the land.

Working as a typist for a yearbook company, I was working a forty-hour plus week. It did bring in more money, but I was so tired! Five months into my pregnancy, I had gained only one pound. Not wanting to admit there might be something wrong, I reassured myself that stress and work were to blame. After all, my OBGYN said the baby's heartbeat was strong!

One of the features in the house I particularly enjoyed was the fireplace. There is very little need in California for a fireplace! There were blowers on both sides to ensure warmth throughout the house. It was frigid the morning I left for work with baby in tow. There were still burning embers in the fireplace, but there was no need to fool with it as I shut the carport door.

Arriving home after work, the house had the distinct odor of ash upon opening the door. Flicking on the lights, there was dark black soot covering every inch of the house. The white kitchen counter tile was now the same black as the grout between the tiles.

Coming up behind me, seeing the black mess, there was no gasp, no *Oh, my gosh*! It was, "What did YOU do? Did you shut the flue?"

He didn't believe me when I denied any knowledge of how it had happened. I had not touched the fireplace! We couldn't stay in the house, the odor was too strong.

The only words he spoke to me were, "Clean it up yourself. I'm not lifting a finger!"

The washing machine ran non-stop for days. Every curtain, drape, bedspread, even the towels in the linen closet had to have the stench of ash washed out. Relatives came to help me with the woodwork and walls. Since I was pregnant, they would not allow me to wash the ceilings. The old wives' tale of not lifting your arms over your head was carried out to a tee.

I was exhausted after days of non-stop cleaning. He came home when he knew the house was clean. The only butterflies I felt were the small movement of the baby within me.

February 2nd broke cold and snowy. Three inches of snow had fallen overnight with predictions of more to come. Not wanting to relinquish the warmth of our bed, I lay perfectly still, trying to ease the pain in my lower back. Begrudgingly, I crawled out of bed.

The cold of the bedroom seemed to make the pain in my back increase in intensity. I was becoming more and more alarmed. "I think I better stay home today, my back really hurts."

Replying, "Oh it probably isn't anything, hurry up and get dressed."

I hurriedly got dressed and left with him. He would take me to work only if the roads were packed with snow and ice.

Snow was coming down hard enough to make the twenty-mile drive even more hazardous. Arriving late, I clung to the step railings to keep from falling.

Grateful I had not fallen on the ice or the water puddle on the floor, I settled in for a long day of typing. Strong contractions soon enveloped me, and I knew instinctively the baby was coming.

Getting the nurse to come to the phone seemed like an eternity. Explaining I wasn't due until May and my contractions were getting closer together, she advised me to get to the hospital as she thought I was in labor.

Calling him at work was frowned upon, but I had no choice. Fearfully, as he answered his extension, I said, "You have to come get me, I'm in labor."

His voice, tinted with anger, told me, "It will take me awhile to get there, be ready."

Cold, shivering, and scared, I sat on the bathroom floor waiting. When I thought enough time had passed, I clutched my stomach and made my way to the parking lot. Finally, I saw his red truck turning into the parking lot. He was obviously annoyed as I got into the passenger seat, but no words were spoken.

The hospital wasn't far by the main roads, but he took the side roads to avoid cars stuck in the snow. Putting his truck into four-wheel drive, he maneuvered a steep hill, slipping sideways. Noticing a car stuck in the ditch, he stopped the truck to help pull it out of the ditch. I couldn't believe it! Labor pains were coming every few minutes and he was acting chivalrous!

Arriving at the hospital, waiting for a wheelchair to take me to the maternity ward, I stood close within his hug and whispered, "I'm scared."

He showed concern for the first time. "It will be alright," faded into the closing of the elevators as he stood in the lobby.

If I could have gotten my legs out of the stirrups, I would have kicked my doctor. "From what I see, the baby has been dead for a few days. You have to be taken to delivery."

In between my cries, I questioned him, "You said she was fine just a week or so ago! What happened?"

He never answered me. Thinking back, my best conclusion was my doctor knew I was going to miscarry and just waited for it to happen without telling me. Delivery this time was not a pleasant or a happy experience. Closing my eyes after the spinal block, I tried to suppress the realization that the baby was gone.

The pressure of the nurse's hands on my stomach woke me. Rhythmic pushing caused me to cry out in pain. "Why are you doing this?"

"Hemorrhaging is a possibility, this is for precautionary measures."

Panic stabbed at my heart. The nurse tried to reassure me, saying she would come back soon. "Soon" meant blood pressure checks and stomach massages every fifteen minutes.

Lying flat without a pillow to prevent headaches from the spinal block, I finally dosed, only to be awakened by the sound of crying babies. Groggy, it didn't dawn on me our baby was gone until I asked where I was. Confusion masked my anger as the nurse stated, 'the maternity ward."

How could the doctor do this? How cruel! New mothers were soothing their infants, whispering soft lullabies. Grief overwhelmed me as I lay there aching for my baby and waiting for him.

What a sad commentary on our life together it was, when my first words to him when he entered my room was, "Please don't leave me."

Guilt made him stay, not love. The baby weighed less than sixteen ounces—a blessing as we didn't have to name her because she wasn't considered "viable." Two ounces more would have required a birth *and* a death certificate. Neither he nor I spoke of who we thought was to blame, until years later.

The next year was awkward between us. Eggs were everywhere I stepped, breaking into tiny pieces. Never knowing when he would be in a good mood or not, I attempted to be the perfect wife and mother, ignoring his remarks, late nights out, and his cold shoulder. Slowly we regained some semblance of a family again. I felt like a Night Butterfly: they have ears on their wings so they can avoid bats. My ears became my wings.

Nineteen seventy-nine brought more changes: the birth of our second child, a son. He was the blessing we needed in our lives.

Butterflies were flying!

We moved north of Nashville to promote his career. Neither he nor I could have ever imagined that what we perceived as a good move, a fresh start, would ultimately be the beginning of our downfall.

We settled comfortably into our new home. We were active in the kids' school activities, church, and sports. We developed a close relationship with a couple that had children the same age as ours. *Best friends* describes the relationship which blossomed between us. Opposites *can* relate to each other. She, the extrovert, would enter a room, cigarette in hand, directing attention to herself. More of an introvert, I stayed on the fringes of conversations. We differed in almost every aspect of our lives.

Meeting in ballet class, our girls became almost inseparable. On the weekend and during the summer they were always together. Our son was born a year and a half before their youngest child. We were there the day their second girl was born on our wedding anniversary.

Our families vacationed together, the beach our usual destination. The first morning, the lapping of the waves woke me early. Rising to enjoy the smell of salt air and to have coffee with him on the balcony, I found them already up talking, my best friend and my husband. The thought of anything going on between the two of them never entered my mind.

***

As the kids grew, our focus was on them. They were our lives. To the outside community, we seemingly had it all: contentment with home, family, and friends. I didn't notice the butterflies were again diminishing more and more. Five years had come and gone, and he was given the opportunity to be groomed for his prize goal of General Manager.

We were moving back to his hometown. We—my best friend and I—sat on our living room floor watching the movers load the remaining furniture. I would miss her, but why was she crying so hard? We would be only one hour away.

Adjusting her sunglasses to leave she said, "I can't take this anymore, I'm going."

To this day, I am not certain if she was crying for him or me!

We moved into the house I thought we would be in until the kids grew up. I'm not sure if he mellowed or had just become complacent. For a while we were happy. We kept in touch with our friends in Gallatin, but we also had new friends. More compatible with our personalities, we became fast friends. Again, our kids were similar in age; they had two boys.

Change comes in increments, sometimes too small to notice, until it explodes into a seemingly endless nightmare. I no longer believed in myself. He had chipped away at my self-esteem over the years. I had allowed this happen. I had heard his disparaging remarks over and over, finally believing them myself. When I looked in the mirror, I didn't see myself; I saw the image of him staring back at me. Whatever accomplishments he earned I took upon myself.

I was gone!

He would tease me in public over the most inconsequential things, and I begged him to stop. He wouldn't. At a church Christmas party, he announced loudly, "Why don't you just put that fudge on your hips? That's where it's going to end up!"

Laughing it off, I defended him, saying he was only teasing. But teasing always has a hint of truth. I was an embarrassment to him. After two children, I no longer had the bikini body, and I was a boring stay-at-home mom, not a career person.

All I was sure of then was the love of our children and my determination to keep us together, to keep up the perfect family image! The new General Manager and president of the Little League, who had a loving wife and children who worshipped him, had to be preserved.

***

Did I hear him correctly? He wanted a *what?* Why, after all these years of struggle, work, and reconciliation? After all, didn't he say we would be all right? How did we get here? I was terrified! I had a high school education, no real work experience, and no self-esteem. How was I going to raise our kids without him? How could I tell them everything would be okay when I didn't believe it myself? He was my rock even though the years had worn away the facade.

I was eighteen when we started this journey, and three weeks away from my fortieth birthday when, on that hot summer night, he left. No smell of sweet orange blossoms, just the wailings of our children. I stood in the doorway watching until I could no longer see the taillights of his car. I could not comprehend how my heart could hurt so badly and I not die. I screamed and no sound came out, only silent agony.

The scene the morning after was beyond my capability to endure. The recliner managed to hold both the kids, clinging to each other for comfort. Rising from the couch, I gathered enough energy to suggest we go for a drive. I'd go see my friend. She was more independent than me. She was stronger, and I needed some of that strength!

We drove north for an hour to the bank where she now worked. My unkempt appearance must have startled her, as she suggested I go home and fix my hair.

I replied, "My husband of twenty-two years just walked out on us, do you really think I care what my hair looks like?"

She couldn't leave work for another hour. The kids and I drove around remembering our lives there, talking, crying, not understanding. We arrived at her house in the early afternoon. I collapsed into a chair, thankful for a refuge from the storm. I didn't want to go home.

"Does he know where you are?" was her first question.

Seemed strange to me it wasn't something like, "How are you handling this?" "I can't believe it!" "Does he know where you are again?"

Upon my answering "no", she forcefully suggested I call and let him know where we were. I refused.

We stayed a while, gathering the courage to return to our empty home. Her husband came in from work just as we were leaving. I remember saying, "Please don't ever be a jerk."

His reply was, "I'm trying really hard not to be," but my fog-induced brain didn't catch it!

She walked us out to the car. Not knowing this would be the last time I would see her as a friend, I was mortified when she said, "Pick yourself up by your boot straps. You and the kids will be fine. You don't need a man in your life." Too tired to figure out what she meant, we drove away.

***

He had moved into a condo, but his telephone bill was delivered to our "home" by mistake. Did I have the right to open it? A little steam and he wouldn't know. I had to know whom he was calling. My eyes and brain didn't register the number at the same time. I barely made it to the bathroom!

They wouldn't do this to me. My husband and my best friend! Flashbacks of her statements popped in my head like popcorn. *That's* why she was crying so hard! Oh, my God, no! How could I have missed the signs? I had gone to her for support and encouragement! I don't believe I could have sunk any further into the depths of humiliation. I laid on the floor sobbing.

No butterflies, just the nauseating feeling welling up within me.

The court date arrived a year after he left. The day lasted forever. I remember him winking at me when, on the stand, she acknowledged their affair. I wanted to leap across the table and beat him with the last ounce of energy I had. But, those crazy butterflies were still there. How could they be? Betrayal from both your husband and best friend is a double edge sword. It was final!

I came to hate the saying, "Get on with your life." What life? The life I had known was gone. I was empty. I clung to the kids like they were my lifesavers.

Over time, the pain turned into unbearable anger. This wasn't me. I'm a Moon Child. I was born under the sign of the crab. I'm family oriented, passive, and dislike conflict. Perhaps, looking back, if I hadn't been so passive and stood up to him, actually argued with him… perhaps he would have had more respect for me, as I would have.

I had to begin to live again. How? The train was moving and I wasn't on it. I couldn't get the words, "You are not pretty enough, smart enough, or good enough for me," out of my head. How could I do anything when he didn't love me or have faith in me?

I was forty-one, scared out of my wits, and questioning my sanity when I walked into that college classroom for the first time since I was eighteen. It seemed a lifetime ago. Walking across the stage three years later to receive my degree, *cum laude*, I had solid proof I was smart enough!

I knew I wasn't the same person. I knew I was stronger than I had given myself credit for. I had survived without him. I was proud of what I had accomplished, who I was, and the positive direction in which I was headed. I saw myself reflecting back in the mirror now. I could see myself reflecting back in the mirror now; not a young, naïve eighteen year old, but a more mature, wiser, and definitely independent woman.

Looking up into the balcony, walking across that graduation stage, I watched my son and daughter give me the "thumbs up!" I knew I had accomplished the greatest goal of all. I was loved and respected by the two treasures in my life. Tears couldn't be held back!

Self-esteem is fleeting, taking nourishment and time to rebuild. I was finally on the train; not necessarily enjoying the ride all the time, but I was moving.

And those butterflies? I know without a doubt, they are gone!

About the author:

Patricia Dainty resides in Sand Springs, Oklahoma with her husband and their three tuxedo cats. Her proudest accomplishment is her two children who have grown into astonishing adults. Patricia holds an AAS degree in Human Services and a BS degree in Sociology; she is currently working towards her Masters degree in Human Relations at

OU/Tulsa. "Butterflies Gone" was her first attempt in writing a short story. Inspired by the success of this story, she plans on writing more short stories and eventually a novella.

CRUEL JUSTICE
©2007 by Bill Westhead

James, clothed in oilskins which he thought appropriate for the occasion, stood on a small, hastily erected wooden platform. It was the summer of 1843 and most of the villagers of Smerton in northern England were gathered around the structure. Unlike James, the men wore boots, corduroy trousers tied with string at the knee, woolen shirts and leather jerkins, while the women sported ankle-length woolen dresses topped with heavy woolen sweaters to protect them from the strong northwesterly wind. James gazed out over the wind-swept sands to the churning Atlantic Ocean beyond, where rolling white caps stretched as far as the mist laden horizon, and thought of George.

Brawny of build with dark hair, James was typical of his Saxon ancestors, while tall, blonde, broad-shouldered George was clearly of Viking descent. The closest of friends, almost family ever since they could remember, they had done everything together. As boys, they had often been seen in the uppermost branches of the same tree, or working the same piece of ground. In their late teens they had rolled the same girls in the hay, played darts and drank in the same pub. By the time the boys were twenty, both sets of parents had left the village for more lucrative jobs in the large town some twenty miles to the north. But James and George decided to stay and, within a year, had built their own small fishing boat with its two sets of oars and single sail. From then on, they spent every day, weather permitting, in the boat, loving the wind in their faces and the tang of the sea air. Their enterprise had proved profitable, particularly when the Lord of the Manor agreed to buy some of their catch.

MIND TRIPS UNLIMITED – 103

Then George announced he was going to marry the village beauty, Anne; she with the black eyes and long dark hair that fell almost to her hand-span waist. James received the news with mixed feelings of hurt and envy. Hurt because, only three months earlier, Anne had turned down *his* marriage proposal claiming to be too young to settle down; and envy that she had, so soon afterwards, yielded to another. In the weeks following, James struggled to accept the situation, but on the day of the wedding he kissed the bride, hugged the groom and genuinely wished them both happiness.

But such was not to be. From the moment Anne entered George's cottage she changed. No longer the happy, self-assured girl, she now feared her husband was about to abandon her in favor of another village girl. Several times a day she would call at the carpenter's shop on one pretext or another to make sure George was there. She would embarrass him in the local pub until he went home with her. If he visited James, she was there in minutes pestering for him to go with her.

Despite this, the friendship between the two men, formed over years, remained steadfast, although circumstances prevented any joint fishing expeditions. Occasionally, James would take the boat out by himself, but fishing had lost its appeal and, more often than not, he could be found laboring on one or other of the surrounding farms.

Early one winter Tuesday morning there was a loud rap on his front door. Surprised that anyone would visit at this hour, James opened it to find George standing there, his blonde hair blowing in the wind, fishing poles in one hand and a bucket of bait in the other.

"Ready?" George asked grinning from ear to ear at the look on James face.

"Where's Anne?" James asked, unable to believe his friend was there without his wife.

"She's at her folk's place. Her mother's sick," George said.

"Well, come on in," James nodded, understanding what had not been said.

"Come in be damned," George said. "I'm here to go fishing not to sit around and talk."

"But look at the weather, lad," James said, pointing to the black clouds rolling in from the sea. "I reckon there's a father and mother of a storm coming up. Come in and let's at least wait a bit until it blows over."

"We've been out in worse," George muttered, glancing skyward as he crossed the threshold. "And if we don't go now, she'll be home and my chance will be lost."

"I understand that," James said, "but I'd rather miss the chance than be caught out there in a storm."

"All right." George gave James a friendly dig in the ribs. "We'll wait a while, but we're going out today no matter what."

They sat together in front of the fire, calloused hands holding pints of home-brewed ale, and waited, neither saying much. By mid-morning George had had enough. Levering himself off the stool, he ambled over to the window. "Yon storm's not getting any worse," he said, gazing upward. "If we don't go soon, I doubt we'll go at all."

Reading the frustration in George's eyes, James reluctantly gathered his gear and, side by side, they made their way down to the boat. The wind blew hard off the sea and a fine spray covered their faces, filling their mouths with the taste of salt. The ever present smell of tar, oakum and paint mingled with that of fish, stirred them as, together, they hauled the boat down the beach.

It took ten minutes of hard rowing to plow through the breaking surf and out into the heavy swell. With the sail raised, they plunged through and over the waves and by early afternoon they had arrived at their favorite fishing spot. The pitching sea made it too dangerous to anchor, so they agreed to take turns, one holding the boat in position while the other fished. Suddenly, George's line tightened and his pole dipped violently.

"Got a winner this time," he shouted above the gale. "Might even be a whale," he added with a grin.

In a few minutes, the line was at its full extent and George, his feet now braced against the gunwale, was leaning back with all his strength. But the fish showed no signs of slowing. Despite the pouring rain and howling wind, George was sweating with exertion as he continued the battle. Remembering whaling stories he had heard, James attempted to turn the bow, so forcing the fish to pull the boat through the water until it tired. But the gale, howling against the sail, made the move impossible and he dared not leave his place at the tiller to try and take the sail in.

"Cut the line!" he yelled, but either George did not hear him or had no means of reaching his knife.

From his strained features and gasping breath, it was clear that

George was losing the fight. As a rogue wave exploded over the boat, his knees buckled. One instant George was fighting the fish and in the next he was over the side, still clinging to the pole. James watched helplessly as his closest friend was dragged through the pounding waves, further and further from safety. Even if George could swim, which James knew he could not, there was no way he would be able to make it back to the boat. In seconds—which seemed to James like hours—George was lost to view in the blinding spray and towering waves.

With glazed eyes, James sat there while the towering waves crashed about him, oblivious to the danger he was in and incapable of taking action to help himself. George had suddenly been taken from him, gone forever, without even a parting word. Tears, mingling with the rain, ran down his face. He felt this had to be as close to death as he would come without dying. Meanwhile, left to its own devices, the boat was tossed about like a small bird in a storm.

The fading daylight seemed to suck the energy out of the storm and, by the time James had recovered enough to bring the boat under control, the gale had lessened to a steady northeaster and the towering waves to a rolling swell. He unlashed two of the oars, reset the tattered sail and headed to shore.

It was pitch black as he made his way up the headland to his stone cottage. Still in a daze, he lit the fire, cast off his soaking wet clothes and stood naked before it. Slowly, his senses began to return and he realized Anne must be wondering where George was. He knew he had to go and tell her the tragic news. But how would he break it to her?

Two hours later, he found himself outside Anne's cottage, although he did not remember how he got there. The place was in darkness as he hammered on the door. Silence. He hammered again and again, each strike more desperate than the one before. Finally, a candle flickered in the window to his right. He heard the door bolt being drawn back and then Anne was standing before him dressed in a long nightshirt, her hair hanging loosely down her back.

"George?" she said, holding the candle up high while her black eyes searched the darkness.

"No, Anne, it's me."

Recognizing James, Anne's voice began to rise in alarm. "Where's George?" she said.

There was no answer. She repeated the question, this time more slowly. Still James could not bring himself to speak. They stood face to face for several moments, the air thick with the unspoken knowledge of regret and loss. Then, of a sudden, Anne dropped the candle. "You've taken him from me," she screamed, rushing at him, fists clenched. James stood there for several minutes feeling nothing as she beat on his chest and face. At last, putting his powerful arms around her he led her back into the cottage.

Once inside, he settled her into a rocking chair by the dying embers while he sat, hunched forward in the spindle-back chair across from her, his elbows on his thighs, his hands hanging between his legs.

After some time James plucked up courage to say, "He's gone, Anne."

Clutching her arms around her, Anne swayed back and forth, intermittent moans from deep within her being the only sound to break the silence. They stayed like that for what seemed hours before exhaustion overtook them, and they fell into a fitful sleep.

Anne awoke as daylight pierced the tiny windows. The sight of James still sitting opposite her brought everything back and she started to wail. James, awakened by the sound, moved to comfort her but she would have none of it.

"What happened?" she said, her voice lifeless as she pushed him away.

In a low, faltering voice James told her everything that had gone on out in the Atlantic Ocean. How, in the first place, he had been reluctant to go fishing with George because of the weather, the fight with the fish and ending with the wave sweeping George overboard. During the whole story, Anne did not speak, although throughout he felt her staring eyes piercing his very soul.

It was not until he had finished, that she said, "Why didn't you try and save him?" Then, seeing the look on his face screamed, "You didn't try, did you? You wanted to take him from me, didn't you?"

It was obvious to James that, in her warped frame of mind, she could not—or would not—understand the terrible plight he had found himself in. He tried again to explain the conditions on the boat and that if he had moved, the boat would undoubtedly have capsized in the storm and both of them would have drowned.

"Perhaps you should have been," she shouted. "You left your

best friend— maybe your only friend—to drown so you could take me. Isn't that it?" She paused, gasping for breath, before adding, "Although you've tried to cover it up, I know you were jealous because I chose George and not you, and yesterday you saw your chance to get even." Then, with a hollow laugh that would have done justice to a witch, added, "Well, you failed. I will kill myself before I'll have anything to do with you, you murderer."

James gasped at the accusation. "That's not true," he shouted. "George was like a brother to me. The brother I never had." He paused and took a deep breath, before saying what he thought had to be said. "From the way you treated George after you were married, I'm thankful you chose him and not me. If it hadn't been for your possessiveness this would never have happened."

They glared at each other for some minutes, neither daring to say more. Then James leaped to his feet and thrust his hands deep into his pockets. "I think I'd better go," he said, staring down at Anne, his face red with rage and embarrassment. "What's more," he added as he reached the door, "after what you've just said, anything that might have been between us is dead. I don't care what you think in that distorted mind of yours, I would have given my bloody life for him if it would have saved him. We went out in that storm because it was the only time he could get away. It was you constantly checking on him that killed him, not me."

He slammed the door behind him.

Although they saw each other often in the village during the next several weeks, neither spoke. At the same time, the locals harbored doubts as to the truth of James' story. They knew he had been fond of Anne, even after she developed her clinging ways, and were not averse to wondering aloud if he might not have pushed George overboard, and then made up the fish story.

James, himself, said nothing to change their minds. Even when George's bloated body washed up on the shore two weeks later with part of the smashed fishing pole still clutched in his hands, the villagers did not change their minds.

The funeral was held in the small church, the women, including Anne, off to one side, sobbing, hands to their mouths, while the men stood silently around the grave, heads bowed. No one spoke to James afterwards, nor did they for the next three months. It was as though he no longer existed. As soon as he entered the village shop, all chatter would cease. The owner, old Mr. Spencer, refused to serve James or even look at him, telling his grandson Robert to attend to the matter, which he did in complete silence. As soon as James left the shop, the chatter would start again. At work on the farm it was the same.

He had no interest in taking the boat out; and so it lay, anchored in the dunes, exactly as he had left it the night of the disaster. In his spare time he either sat alone in his cottage or on the beach, staring out to sea. No matter where he was and no matter how hard he tried, he could not get his last sight of George out of his mind. It was there on the beach that Anne found him one morning in early spring.

"James," she shouted as she came over the dunes and saw him. "I need to talk to you."

There was no answer. It seemed as though he had not heard her.

"Are you still grieving for George?" she continued, sitting down beside him and following his gaze. Still he did not answer. "Or are you wondering whether or not to take the boat out again?"

At mention of the boat, he turned to look at her and for the first time noticed how much weight she had put on; yet her face was drawn and matted hair hung down her back as though it had not seen a comb for months. The weight did not suit her and he suddenly realized that she might be pregnant with a child George would never see. Still, he could not bring himself to speak. Together they stared out to sea, the silence between them broken only by the sound of the waves swishing up the shore.

"Why are you, of all people, suddenly talking to me? No one else will," he finally said. "Have you come to your senses at last?"

"I suppose I have," she said, her voice so low James had to lean towards her to hear. "I'm sorry I said what I did. I know it was an accident. "

"Then why don't you tell these fools around here?"

"I will. I promise I will."

"I can't bring him back, Anne," James said, his voice heavy with remorse as tears began to trickle down his cheeks. "I wish to God it had been me and not George." He looked at her pointedly before adding, "Then he would be here for his family."

"Yes, but at least I have something to remember him by," Anne said, patting her enlarged waistline "I know I don't deserve it but I want to know if you will do something for me?"

"What?"

"Will you take me out to the place where it happened, so I can see it for myself?"

James' face paled. The idea of taking the boat out again appalled him and the last place he wanted to go was back to the scene of the tragedy. But, as he looked at her pleading eyes he knew he had no choice. Whatever he might think of her, he felt compelled to do as she asked. After all, this was his best friend's widow. He would do it for George and, at the same time, face his own demons.

He nodded. "Tomorrow, if the weather is fine," he said.

Anne struggled to her feet. "Why not now?" she asked. "The weather's perfect, the sea calm and we'll be back well before dusk. Let me pick some flowers to throw on the place where he took his last breath. I'll be back in an hour."

James looked up at her. He still hated the thought of being in the boat again, but maybe the sooner this was over the better. "All right, we'll go when you get back, although I don't mind admitting I hate the idea."

"I know that," she said, "but maybe it'll help you as much as me."

James nodded. "Maybe," he said.

Anne left to pick her flowers. James stayed where he was for some time before hauling the boat down to the water's edge.

True to her word, Anne returned within the hour, her arms filled with a bunch of wild daffodils. He helped her into the boat and seated her up in the bow while he hoisted the sail. Settling back, he pulled steadily on the oars. Arriving at the site of the disaster, as near as he could recall, James shipped the oars, leaned back and gazed across the calm seas, thinking of the storm that had been so costly to both of them.

"This is it," he finally said.

They sat in silence for some minutes, each lost in thought. Then Anne rose slowly and stepped to the middle of the boat. With one foot on the gunwale, to steady herself against the rocking motion, she turned in his direction. James was surprised to see those black eyes which, only hours ago, had been soft and beseeching now stared through him at something only Anne could see. He watched her through eyes blurred with tears, fascinated by this strange look which he had never seen before.

She raised her arms as if to throw the flowers into the sea, looked skywards and, in a low voice, said "I'm coming, George." Before James could move, she leaped over the side, the daffodils still clutched to her bosom.

"Anne!" he screamed as he staggered forward and dived in after her.

The water was clear and he could see her sliding down into the depths. Her skirt, tightly wrapped around her, coupled with her tendril-like hair, gave her the appearance of a sea serpent. Making no effort to save herself, she continued to clutch the flowers, their yellow petals breaking away and forming a halo round her dark head. She was well below him and he kicked violently in an effort to reach her, but to no avail. Lungs bursting, he broke the surface, took a deep breath and dived again and again and again, each time a little deeper. By his fourth attempt, the stream of air bubbles rising from below had stopped and he realized he had no hope of saving Anne. He clung to the side of the boat until his breathing returned to normal and he could climb aboard.

James sat there wondering at the turn of events. It dawned on him that Anne had intended, all along, to join George by drowning herself and, Lord help him, he had unwittingly helped her do it. Her enlarged figure had not been due to pregnancy, but to weights tied around her waist causing her to sink so rapidly it had been impossible to save her.

Twice now he had been asked to take the boat out against his better judgment and twice the result had been death by drowning. Anne's last words rang in his ears and James realized her sacrifice showed how ardent her love had been for George and how deep-seated her fear of rejection. It was clearly a love he did not have the courage to equal. Anne had deservedly won George and there was nothing James could do to change that, nor was he now even sure he wanted to.

A beaten man, he turned the boat around and headed for shore. Although sweat poured down his face, he shivered and a wet chill climbed the back of his neck at the thought of what awaited him. The villagers had never believed what had happened to George, so it was not difficult to imagine their reaction to his account of Anne's suicide. At best he would be driven from the village, the only place he had ever known.

He pulled the boat back up into the dunes and set out for Anne's parent's cottage. Waiting to deliver the tragic news would only make things worse.

Anne's father, Sam, had already heard his daughter had gone out in the boat with James. Now he stood at his cottage gate, feet apart, muscular arms crossed over his chest and watched James trudge up the lane. The look on James' face as he stopped in front of him told Sam all he needed to know. His heavy fist slammed into the young man's midriff while the other crashed into his jaw. Taken totally unawares, James dropped like a felled tree.

He came around to find himself lying on the floor of the village jail, a group of locals silently glaring at him through the heavy iron bars. There was no point in trying to explain, he could clearly see the hatred in their eyes. Stumbling over to a urine-stained, straw-filled mattress in the corner, he threw himself down, facing the granite stone wall and ignored them.

Three weeks later, the village brought him to trial on two charges of murder. As James entered the small, crowded courtroom, he noticed George's parents sitting in the front row staring at him. He turned away, unable to meet their look of sorrow and disbelief. He wished his own parents could have been there to speak on his behalf, but after his mother's death three years ago, his father had sailed to Ireland and James had not heard from him since.

The trial was short and swift, the visiting judge having only one day for the village court before riding on to the next town. The prosecution called three people to testify: Anne's father and mother and George's father. Although no one had witnessed either event, all three gave it as their opinion that James had drowned George in order to marry Anne and when she refused him he drowned her.

James had no one to speak in his defense except himself. Again he told the story of the fishing accident, pointing out as proof he was telling the truth that George was still gripping the shattered pole when his body was washed ashore. He was encouraged by sympathetic nods from some of the jurors.

But when it came to Anne's death, his story met with stony silence. Her parents pointed out that, despite a thorough search of her cottage, no suicide note had been found and that on the day in question she was her usual cheery self. It was, therefore, highly unlikely, they argued, that she would jump overboard as James claimed. He had no answer.

It took the jury thirty minutes to return their verdict. James sighed with relief when they found him not guilty of killing George. But that relief was short lived, for in the next breath the foreman announced him guilty of drowning Anne.

The judge pronounced sentence and James wept as he was led back to his cell.

Now James stood on that hastily erected platform, staring out to sea. If he looked over to his left, he could just see the mast of his boat, the unwitting source of all his troubles, protruding above the dunes. Suddenly, he felt arms around his shoulders and sensed he was not alone. Glancing sideways, he saw tall, blond George to his right and dark-haired Anne to his left. As he stretched his arms out to embrace his friends, Anne's father pulled the lever and the floor of the platform dropped away. James felt no pain as his body plummeted into space, only a profound thankfulness that the three of them were, at last, together again.

About the author:

Born in Clitheroe, England, and educated at Rossall School, Bill Westhead graduated from Leeds University with an honors degree in Textile Engineering. He is the fourth generation of his family to work in the textile industry.

After service in the British Army, he worked in the synthetic fiber industry in Wales, England and Northern Ireland. In 1973 he and his family emigrated to Waycross, Georgia where as Vice President/Company Director, he was primarily responsible for the design and development of heavy industrial fabrics for use in the manufacture of paper.

A member of Southeastern Writers Association and Coastal Writers Group he has published four historical novels, 'Once in Old Frederica Town' (1993), 'Clogs' (1999), Confederate Gold' (2002) and 'The Mill', a sequel to 'Clogs' (2005). All four novels continue to be available on Amazon.com. He is also the author of several short stories published in 'Cricket', 'Animal Tales' and 'Chicken Soup for the Dog Lover's Soul' as well as non-fiction articles in 'Crafts 'n Things' and a number of trade magazines.

His short story 'Romeo and Sierra's Last Mission' was also a winner in the 2005 Scribes Valley contest and published in 'They Do Exist!'

Currently, he is working on his fifth novel while, at the same time, writing a monthly theater column 'Footlights' for the Waycross Journal Herald.

When not writing, he divides his time between working on his Bonsai collection and the Waycross Area Community Theatre where, over a number of years, he has undertaken every aspect of local theater from acting and directing to sweeping out the house.

He can be contacted at westhead@accessatc.net.

A ROYAL VISIT
©2007 by Donna Bryant

Mama and Aunt Dee said that I was too young to remember him 'cause I had only been two years old the last time that my Uncle had come to visit. But they told me that I was gonna love him to death 'cause everybody was crazy about Uncle Royal B. For weeks, Uncle Royal B was all anybody in my house talked about or thought about. It seemed to me that Uncle Royal B was gonna be special to me 'cause, just like me, he had a different than usual name. At least that's what everybody told me—that I just didn't fit my name—that I didn't look like a Meredith Daugherty.

"I bet it's been at least five years since Baby Brother was last here," said Mama.

"Nope, it's been exactly six and a half years come this fall," said Aunt Dee as she reached across the table for another helping of mashed potatoes that, according to Daddy, she really didn't need.

"Royal B," Aunt Dee said, smiling, dreamily. She shook her head so that the auburn curls of her brand-new wig swung back and forth across her face. She leaned way forward, grinned her big toothy grin at me and tapped her shiny acrylic nails on the table.

"You know, Baby Girl, we call him Royal B 'cause when he was just a little something or another that boy used to get a hold of a jar of Royal Bee Petroleum Jelly and he would plaster that mess all over his head." Her and Mama fell against each other laughing. "Child, that boy's head would be so sticky and greasy that your Grandma had to pour Tide detergent on his head to get all the grease out."

Daddy snorted and gave Aunt Dee the evil eye as she reached across the table for another pork chop. "So, Evelyn, when exactly is

Roland coming?" he asked Mama.

"Roland?" I asked.

"Yep…Roland." Daddy shook his head and snickered. "See, Baby Girl, *Roland* Watson is your uncle's real name. Ain't nobody but your Mama and Aunt Dee silly enough to call a grown man some stupid name like Royal B."

Mama sighed the way she always did when Daddy was being unreasonable, or as Aunt Dee put it: being a pain in the butt. Her and Aunt Dee rolled their eyes at each other as she told Daddy that Uncle Royal B's bus got in at four o'clock.

Daddy sputtered and almost spit his iced tea all the way across the table. "Four o'clock in the morning! You mean I got to get up out my bed in the middle of the dang-gone night to go get that big old grease-bag—how come he can't catch a cab like a normal person?"

Aunt Dee sucked her teeth real hard and shook her curls away from her face. "You know what, Marcus? If you wasn't so stingy and would let me drive your precious car, then I could go get Baby Brother myself." She threw her napkin on the table in disgust. "You act like that car is made out of gold or something. Matter of fact, you got Evelyn so scared she gonna do something to that car that she probably ain't never gonna learn how to drive."

Daddy pushed his plate back and leaned way back in his chair, and I figured that it wasn't a good sign when Daddy got upset enough to stop eating. "Listen here, Dee," he told her, "If you think for a second that I'm bout to let you and your crazy brother go gallivanting around in my car in the middle of the night, you'd better think again." He shook his finger at both Mama and Aunt Dee. "And don't neither one of y'all think that I done forgot about that crazy mess he pulled the last time he was here."

Daddy rubbed his head like he was fixing to get one of his headaches. "Shoot! That crazy Roland ain't got no more sense than a bedbug."

Mama and Aunt Dee looked at each other and rolled their eyes again 'cause you couldn't do nothing but sit back and relax when Daddy got on a roll. And Daddy could really get on a roll when he got started on Mama's family, 'cause he said they was all crazy as loons. Daddy was always warning Mama that most men wouldn't put up with half the shenanigans that he had to put up with. He said that any other man would have gave up on Mama's crazy family and run off to

China or Timbuktu or someplace and never came back. Daddy said the only reason he didn't run off no place was 'cause he was just a good-hearted and patient man, and Mama was so lucky to have somebody like him. But Daddy said that last time Uncle Royal B had came to visit, he hadn't done nothing but eat and sleep all day long, and it was enough to try the patience of the Pope himself.

Daddy puffed up his chest the way he always did when he got ready to tell a long story. "See, Baby Girl, I had been nice enough to let old Roland stay up in my house for two weeks or more, and then I come home early one day to get me some peach cobbler that your Mama had made." He sighed for a minute and got a faraway look in his eyes as he got to thinking about Mama's peach cobbler. "I had hid a little dish of it way back in the back of the refrigerator 'cause you know if I don't hide me a little something every now and then, I can't hardly get a crumb of food in my own house." He gave Aunt Dee a look when he said that, but she just looked up at the ceiling like she wasn't paying him no mind.

"But, by the time I got home that day, some greedy-gut had found my cobbler and ate it all up." Daddy shook his head, and he looked even sadder about that cobbler than he did when he had accidently run down our dog Rufus in the driveway the year before. Daddy had said that he was sorry about Rufus being dead and all, but he also said that Rufus didn't have no dang business being in the driveway in the first place. And no!—we couldn't get no more dogs 'cause he didn't have time to be always looking over his shoulder for some stupid dog in the driveway. Anyway, Daddy said his cobbler disappearing like that had just been the last straw and he figured it was about time for him and Roland to have them a little man-to-man talk.

Daddy cleared his throat and pushed his chair back a little more so he could stretch his legs and give himself some more belly room. Mama and Aunt Dee looked like they wished they was maybe on the moon, or anyplace else other than having to sit there and listen to Daddy tell his story.

"So then I headed upstairs to tell that boy a thang or two about how you supposed to act when you staying in somebody's house...like not staying in the bathroom for two hours when folks got to get ready for work, and not leaving your stanking socks laying all over. The kind of stuff that his parents should of told him if they had raised him right."

Daddy put his hand up in the air like the school crossing guard when Aunt Dee acted like she was fixing to say something. "But when I got upstairs, there was that son-of-a-giraffe laying up in my bed as naked as the day is long! Big, rusty butt propped up on my favorite blanket, and on the phone running up my long distance bill to boot!" Daddy had to stop to catch his breath and he took a long sip of iced tea, and I could see that nerve jumping in his left eye the way it always did when he got to talking about Mama's family.

"Baby Girl, I tell you, I've always done everything I could to help out your Uncle Roland, but you know, right is right and wrong is wrong, and there wasn't nothing right about that fool laying buck-naked in my bed. So I sent him to his room to put on some draws, and then I nicely suggested that it might be a good idea for him to go visit your Uncle Raymond up in Michigan for a while." Then Daddy settled back in his chair and let out a long sigh like he had just finished running a good race, but Aunt Dee shot up out of her chair so quick that for a minute I thought the house might be on fire.

"I'll be dang, Marcus," she hollered. "How can you sit there and tell that rat-faced lie?" She got to walking around the table in circles and waving her arms in the air like she was ready to testify in church or something. Then she stopped in front of Daddy and pointed her razor-sharp nails at him. "You know what, Brother-in-law? You better hope and pray that the Lord don't strike you right out your shoes for lying 'cause you know you ain't never suggested nothing *nicely* to Royal B or anybody else in this family."

Well, after that, her and Daddy got to fussing back and forth like they always did, but I didn't pay much attention 'cause I knew they could go on forever about who was lying and who was crazy and so on. I really just wanted to go upstairs where it was quiet and peaceful so I could think about how much fun it was going to be when Uncle Royal B came to visit. I couldn't wait till we could go together and sit in the park on Saturday mornings and feed the birds and watch kids go by on their skates and Roller Blades. And on warm nights we could sit out on the porch in the light of the moon, eating bowls of Mama's homemade peach ice cream while we watch fireflies dance in the dark. And maybe one night when it is peaceful and quiet, I might get a chance to tell Uncle Royal B a few of the things that I really want to get off my chest. Like how I was always thinking of traveling to faraway places. I figured that I could be one of those airline stewardesses who get to travel to places like France or Egypt or Japan. I was gonna tell him stuff like that, stuff that I never got a chance to tell nobody else. I hoped he wouldn't laugh when I told him that I still believed, sometimes late at night, that there was a monster hiding up under my bed. And I planned to make him swear not to ever tell anybody else about how cute Tommy Carter was, and how he had told me I had really pretty eyes.

'Cause I just knew without a doubt that with everybody saying how nice and fun Uncle Royal B was, that me and him was gonna be the best of friends, and he would probably want to spend most of his time with me seeing as how I was his one and only niece in the whole wide world.

After dinner was over that night and Daddy had stomped off to sulk in front of the TV, me and Mama and Aunt Dee was cleaning up the kitchen. Then Aunt Dee turned on the radio and started acting like we was having a party or something. Every time a good song came on the radio, she'd jump in the middle of the floor and start dancing and telling Mama to come on and shake her thang. Mama would laugh and wave her hand and tell Aunt Dee to stop her foolishness 'cause they was way too old to be acting like that. But Aunt Dee would pull her out in the middle of the floor and they would do some of those old time dances that they liked to do. Then Mama told Aunt Dee that with that red wig on her head she was just the spitting image of Tina Turner when she sang that "Rollin' on the River" song. And Aunt Dee threw her head back, laughed and shook her curls and told Mama she needed to just shut her mouth.

The morning that Uncle Royal B came to visit, I woke up with the same feeling that you get on Christmas mornings when you can't wait to jump out of bed so you can get the day started. I hurried to get washed and dressed and I was real careful to wash all my parts and make sure my clothes was clean and matched so that Mama wouldn't have no reason to send me back upstairs. Plus, I wanted to look good for my Uncle Royal B, seeing as how he had traveled all this way to see me. I figured that the least I could do was put my best foot forward like Mama was always telling me.

Downstairs, Mama was playing the radio loud and stirring pancake batter and singing along with old songs like "I Heard it through the Grapevine" and "Ain't No Mountain High Enough" by Miss Diana Ross. There was Uncle Royal B big as day, sitting in the breakfast nook reading the newspaper. At first I didn't know what to think of him except I guess he was what people mean when they say that somebody is stout…or rotund…which was one of the words that I missed in the spelling bee last spring. His shirt was wrinkled and had old food stains on it, and he had it buttoned up all wrong like he wasn't nothing but a big old kid that didn't even know how to dress hisself. He had a big, round face with skin so loose that it quivered like Jell-O does when you touch the bowl and set it in motion. His eyes were big and round, and real black, and they moved around a lot like he was always trying to look at everything at once.

He looked over and saw me standing in the doorway and it was like he couldn't figure out who I was or where a little girl like me could have come from. But then he forgot about me real quick when Mama set a plate of golden-brown pancakes in front of him.

"Here you go, Baby Boy, I put real buttermilk in these pancakes."

Uncle Royal B hunched way over his plate, and he reminded me of the way old Rufus would hunch over his food and gobble it down back before Daddy ran him down in the driveway.

With his mouth all full of pancakes, Royal B managed to say, "Dang, Evelyn, you know I sure have missed your cooking. Matter of fact, the only reason I even came to visit was 'cause I just couldn't stay away from your cooking one minute longer."

Big globs of sweat was pouring down his face while he ate and mixing with the syrup and butter that was streaking down his chin. His round, black eyes were rolling around like marbles gone wild as he shoveled those pancakes into his mouth. Then he looked over and saw me still standing in the doorway.

"You know, Evelyn," he said, "I never did understand why you went and named that child Meredith. What kind of name is Meredith for a little black girl? Shoulda gave her a normal name like Tanya or Yolanda or something." His eyes slid over me for a second, then he sat back, belched and motioned for Mama to bring more pancakes, sausages and eggs.

I don't know how long I stood in that doorway, but finally Mama told me to quit acting gumpy and say hello to my uncle like I had good sense. I spoke to him the way I had been taught to speak to adults but all he did was grunt and keep right on eating. I slunk away to go sit on the back porch and watch baby squirrels learn how to find nuts and race back up the tree trunks with them tucked away in their jaws.

A ladybug landed on my knee and I watched her wave her antennas around wildly like she was trying desperately to figure out where she was. My science teacher had said that most bugs used their antenna to see, they didn't see with their eyes like people do. I figured that it was like walking into a dark room and feeling your way around with your hands. You had a funny feeling in your stomach until you touched something that you recognized like the edge of the dresser or the closet door and then you knew exactly where you were and what to do next. So I got down on my knees so that ladybug could fall off my leg into the grass. I knew once she felt those grass blades with her antenna, she'd know exactly where she was and from there she could find her way home.

I stayed in the backyard for a long time that day 'cause, like the ladybug, I needed to sort of feel my way and figure some things out. Aunt Dee had come in from her job at the factory and I could hear her and Mama and Uncle Royal B laughing and cackling like there wasn't nobody else on the face of the whole earth except the three of them. I figured that Mama would call me in to eat lunch at some point, but they must of been so caught up in their good times that nobody even gave me a thought. I decided that I'd stay out there till Daddy came home 'cause of course *he* would miss me. I imagined him saying to Mama, "Hey, where is my Baby Girl done gone to? You know I got to see my Meredith as soon as I get home."

But then nature was having its way with me and I had to go inside to take care of business. Maybe it was for the best anyway 'cause I got to thinking that with all the hoopla of Royal B visiting and all, that maybe even Daddy might forget about his Baby Girl. So in the end I figured it was best if I went inside before Daddy got home 'cause that way he wouldn't have to worry about remembering me since he had a lot on his plate already.

In the house, Royal B was sitting at the head of the table and Mama and Aunt Dee was standing around him. It reminded me of those movies where there's a king sitting on a throne and everybody's standing around fanning him with big palm leaves and feeding him grapes. Matter of fact, Aunt Dee was standing there holding a plate of cheese out to him, and Mama reached over and wiped something off his face with a napkin.

I stood there watching them and it felt like I was in one of those Twilight Zone shows. Then Aunt Dee looked around and got to fussing at me about staring. Said it was downright rude for children to stare and I shoulda known better. Then Royal B looked at me like I was a fly that was fixing to fall into his soup. As I stood there, all of a sudden he made me think about the monster that lived under my bed at night. I had never seen the monster—I don't think any kid ever had—but I still knew what he looked like. The scariest part about the monster was always his eyes. Round, mean, ugly eyes. That's what Royal B reminded me of.

That night at dinner, Mama and Aunt Dee looked out for Royal B. "Baby Brother, you got enough of this or that?"; "Sure you don't want some more iced tea?"

Even Daddy seemed like he was trying to be as nice as he could: "So, Roland what's new in your part of the world?"

He didn't even seem to mind when Royal B just humped his shoulder and gave his usual grunt and kept right on eating. Daddy had gave me a half-smile and he winked at me a time or two, but he mostly kept his eyes on either his plate or on Royal B. I knew Daddy was just waiting for him to make a wrong move and then out he would go.

I sat back and, just like always, I didn't open my mouth unless someone spoke to me; and nobody did 'cause they all wanted to talk to Royal B. I wondered just like Daddy how long Royal B was gonna hang around. It wasn't nice and it wasn't the right thing for a kid to say, but I wanted him gone. Not 'cause of all the attention that he got—though that bothered me a little bit, too. But it was mostly 'cause it seemed like I couldn't think with him around. I wanted to go back to my daydreams of flying in silver-blue airplanes to places where lots of yellow poppies grow. I wanted to dream of growing up and wearing glass slippers like the princess in the fairy tales, and have a prince named Tommy kiss me and carry me off in a coach driven by white horses. I'd live in a stone castle on a high hill and get married to Tommy, and change my name to Corrine Carter, and everyone would just love me to death.

About the author:

Donna Bryant was born and raised in Cleveland, Ohio. She is currently in her senior year as an English major at Cleveland State University. She has been writing short stories for many years, and will apply for her MFA within the next year. Donna won first prize in Cleveland State creative writing competitions in 2005 and 2006. She enjoys reading short stories and novels, watching classic movies, and traveling and meeting new people. She hopes to complete a novel very soon.

CORRIDO
©2007 by Bobby Ozuna

A fisherman was singing a song. He was singing a song as though he were singing the very history of his life. He was old, older than his years, weathered by the experiences of a life spent so intimately in poverty. His eyes were sad and heavy, and to look upon them, one could see and feel the traces of a life suffered in service to those he loved—a life of sacrifice. The sky had cast a shadow upon him as though he had paid his dues in labor over many years under the scorching heat of south Texas, as if somehow the brutality of the sun could no longer cause him any discomfort. His life and his labor had become synonymous with pain. He was sitting outside a small framed house in the land where he was raised, the valley—*El Valle.*

This land where he was born, where he had worked and labored to produce a life for a family that has long moved on, had become his heart's blood, and he and the city on the border—by the sea—were one and the same. They were old, he and this land, both rooted in tradition, full of tales, stripped away of all their glorious past in lieu of only memories, memories of better times. His story and the stories of old Mexico—tales of a life and the life of that sacred land—cannot be found in storybooks or fancy bindings, but rather sung, sung just as the stories of others who have passed away without any significance for a lifetime spent on Earth.

He was sitting outside his house on an old paint bucket. His name was Don Fidel Cristiano and he was a fisherman.

With calloused hands he labored diligently to clean an antiquated steel fishing reel, working to wash the corrosive saltwater from its chassis. And there, alone with only his memories and his imagination, he sang a song. He sang a song of loss, of love lost, and he sang a song of death.

A young man many years his junior took his place beside the old man, working to shield his eyes from the penetrating sun. He took a seat beside Don Fidel on an empty paint bucket and he waited for the old man to finish singing. The house was old and the ground was seared, scorched and dying and his porch smelt of fish and traces of bleached water. When he felt the time was right, appreciating the passion of the song, he asked the fisherman to tell him what he was singing about. He asked because the song was in Spanish and because he did not yet fully understand the language.

"What are you singing?"

The old man did not pause to explain, instead he continued on, attentively working to clean his fishing reel as though it were his only possession to show in his life for all his years of hard work.

"*La cancion?*" the young man asked again. The song? "What is the song, *señor?*"

When the fisherman stopped singing, he took from his back pocket an old rag and he wiped the sweat from his face and left it to rest upon his neck, never taking his eyes off the shiny reel. He brought it in closer to his face, blowing into it, ensuring no dust or dirt or composites were left behind. Perfect. The oily smell of the lubricant blew back into his face.

"*La cancion?*" the young man asked again. "What is it about?"

Don Fidel turned to face the young boy and, although his eyes were sad, something in his expression let his visitor know that he was pleased with his arrival. Instead of answering, he posed a question in return. "*Tu eres un autor de historias, verdad?*" He wanted to know if the boy was a writer—a storyteller.

"*Si,*" The young man told him that he was.

"*De donde recibes las ideas para tus historias?*" Don Fidel gathered his thoughts together in his head and asked again. "Nino, where do your stories come from?"

The young man thought about his response, believing as though he might be outwitted by only telling the truth. "From here," he said, pointing to his head. Uncertain how to say his *mind*, he said instead, "*Mi cabesa.*"

The fisherman lit a cigarette and, after inhaling the smoke, he laughed and began to cough; he coughed up phlegm into the very rag he used to wipe his forehead and neck. "They do not come from your head."

"I meant my mind. My imagination, you know?"

The old man said to him in both Spanish and English that one has to have tasted the water from a well before he can speak of it, and that to write of such things as the world has to offer, you first have to be willing to offer up your soul to the world and the world beyond that. He said that only in the service of offering your soul can you begin to understand and appreciate the silent whispers of those souls who have suffered in life before you.

He blew cigarette smoke towards the wind, watching as it broke and scattered in the air. He continued, "This land was once Mexico. Here, *aqui*," he said directing the boy's attention towards the ground with a long, bony finger. "When my father was born, this was Mexico and now the land belongs to *Tejas*. To Texas, *entiendes?*"

The young man agreed with a nod of his head, careful not to appear as though he knew or understood more than his friend. He waited for the old man to inhale another drag of his cigarette. "I'm listening."

"*Bien, bien.*" Good. "And now the land no longer belongs to Mexico. It has been many years since, and she has tasted the loss of many people who have come and gone, lived and died, right here where we sit."

Don Fidel looked around and spanned their surroundings and, pleased with the setting and his tale thus far, he continued. "And to appreciate this simple message, this simple truth, is to respect the silent cries from those who have come before us. They know the truth of the world and they pity us for being so lost, so confused, and they cry out in the wind and they sing to the souls of those who still have something to offer the world." The fisherman found the young man's eyes and said, "You are lucky."

The young man thought of what was being said to him, considering the significance of how and why he wrote the stories he did. "*Con permiso?*" he asked. And with the fisherman's permission he reached for a cigarette from an old cigar box and studied it for a moment. It was short and thick, packed heavily with tobacco. Don Fidel always preferred to roll his own smokes.

The young man lit it and coughed, recognizing the stoutness. "Damn, these are potent." Realizing his friend did not understand the word *potent*, he said instead, "They are strong."

The old man laughed and told the boy that he appreciated his company sometimes more than fishing. He said that fishing in the ocean was always exciting, even after so many years of living that lifestyle, because once your bait is taken, you never can tell what you will get until you reel in your line. And he said that sitting with the boy under the sun was the same for him. He never knew what he might ask or what silly antic he might perform and that always made him smile.

"So are you saying the stories that I see and hear in my mind, in my head, are really the voices of those who came before me? From people who died?"

Don Fidel had already begun reassembling his reel, carefully placing it back onto the long fishing pole. "*Sí, sí.*" Yes. "The same is with the songs of Mexico, the *corridos* we sing. They are the stories of those who have suffered and those who were willing to sacrifice themselves, allowing their lives to become part of the loss that was suffered in the past. To do justice to them, we sing. We sing to forever honor their loss."

The boy puffed on his cigarette and he, too, blew smoke into the wind, watching as it broke and faded away.

"It is the ocean that forms the winds of the world and it is on the wind that the stories are carried, traveling from far away, and others not so far." The fisherman pointed to a nearby palm tree, bit on the end of a cigarette and said, "Listen to them clap and listen to them laugh in the leaves as they blow in the breeze. Listen to the cries within the rain and appreciate their anger in the cracks of the thunder. You have to be still long enough to understand."

Don Fidel reached down and scooped a handful of dirt into his palm and, letting it fall slowly from his hand and scatter into the wind, he said in Spanish, "*De cenias llegamos, a cenias regresaremos.*" From ashes we come, from ashes we will return. "That is where the stories of this world come from. That is where the *corridos* come from, like the one you heard me singing. They are songs of loss, but mostly of death. And we sing them in honor of those who have gone before us, understanding that we can suffer their same fate if we don't listen to what they have to say."

"How do I know my stories come from my soul and not my imagination?"

The fisherman laughed and nodded his head in approval. "Good. You will know after you realize that they do not come from your mind, ever. That not all your abilities come from your own intelligence," he said patting the young man on the head. In Spanish, he told him, "Sure you can write, but to tell a story that has meaning, one that has a purpose, it has to come from your soul. And when you learn to listen to the souls of our past, it is then you will understand your purpose as a writer."

The young man stood, tossing a rock away from where the two of them sat and he watched as it scattered dirt and debris into the air. He began to feel unsure of himself, less confident in his willingness to tell the world that he was a writer, and he tried to apply his lesson to his own life. He stood in disbelief and he felt like a child who may have learned that his childhood hero was fictitious, or worse, that his desires to become something more than those around him, or greater than the world in which he lived, was only a dream that could never be touched or tasted, only imagined within the mind. And worse, he thought perhaps the life he envisioned for himself would only exist on paper, and that caused his heart to ache.

Seeing that the young man was discouraged by his tale, Don Fidel said to him, "*Vamos.* Come on my friend, let's go fishing."

The young man did not move. "Wait. *Esperate, por favor.*"

"*Que haces mi amigo?*"

"Is my writing real?" the boy asked, looking into the sad eyes of the old fisherman. "What I mean is, how will I really know when I am writing from my soul and not from my own mind? How will I know that my writing is pure? That it is true?"

"*Ayudame,*" Don Fidel said, raising one calloused hand into the air, asking the young man to help him back onto his feet. When he stood, he stared directly into the young man's eyes and said, "When you hear the whispers that keep you awake at night, the voices you hear in your head. The ones that won't let you sleep and at times even scare you, and they make you uncomfortable until you get out of bed to write. And when you do sit down to write, late at night, when all the world is still asleep and the stories seem to flow as though they were only waiting to be written, then you will know that it is pure. That it is real."

The boy nodded and succumbed to accept this possible fate, hoping he understood, and wishing to know his own truth about his passion.

"*Andale, vamanos.* It is time for us to go fishing."

The young man collected himself and set his rod and reels into the back of Don Fidel's truck, then he helped his friend to gather their tackle and bait and he started up the truck.

"I will drive today," Don Fidel said, waving the young boy over towards the other end of the bench seat.

Before climbing over to the passenger side, the boy asked again, "Okay, but now will you tell me about the song you were singing?"

"*Si nino,* I will tell you." Don Fidel smiled.

The two of them drove away from the old frame house that had once belonged to the fisherman's father. They eased away from the neighborhood where many children were playing in the street. They were playing soccer in a large dirt field with a frayed leather ball; some of the children were barefoot and others had no shirts, and they smiled and waved to them as they passed. A little girl sat on the curb with a blonde-haired doll cradled in her arms and she was crying. A woman was setting her clothes out to dry on a clothes-line and men were working the cotton fields, their faces hidden beneath wide-brimmed cowboy hats.

The two of them drove on, heading towards the water, and the fisherman told the story of the *corrido* he was singing. The story was a tale of loss, of a mother and father who lost a daughter many years ago. The *corrido* tells of a truck driver who passed along a road known in Mexico as *la curva de muerte*—the curve of death. It was called this because of how the road wound up and around a mountain, then down again on the other side in a snake-like pattern.

The story begins with a truck driver passing through the winding road one night while it was raining. The trucker noticed a lovely young girl, most likely in her early twenties, standing in the rain. Curious, he pulled over to see if she was okay because he did not see a vehicle in the immediate area. She said she was having car trouble and asked him for a ride to her home at the top of the mountain. The driver obliged and delivered her to a gravel road at the end of her parent's property. She then asked if she could inconvenience him again: could he pick her up on the way back down? He said he would not be coming back for a few days, and she said that would be a perfect time to leave. She said she would wait for him and the truck driver drove away.

Days later, the driver did return. He returned to honor his promise to the lovely young lady who needed his help. When he came to the lot where her parents lived, he waited. He parked his rig on the side of the road and the lovely young girl did not come out. At first he thought himself foolish for believing a lovely young girl would wait to ride in the company of a man who worked such a dirty job, or ride in the cab of such a dirty truck. Surely someone would have helped her by now, someone in her family: a boyfriend? A neighbor?

He then considered leaving, but felt sad remembering how much she appreciated his help just days before in the rain. What if she actually needed his help and was waiting for the day when his rig parked outside her parent's house? Some time passed—only minutes not hours—but within that time he noticed people off in the distance, in the house, watching him and, worried that he might cause some confusion or panic, he walked the distance to her home.

With his hat in his hand, as not to cause any alarm, he knocked and was immediately greeted by a lady much older than he, possibly the young girl's grandmother. He introduced himself and said he was there to honor a promise to the girl, to take her back to her car. He was asked to come inside and was introduced to an old man who said he was the young girl's father.

Both the girl's parents were old, much older than any individuals who might appear to have a daughter in the youth of her life. They asked the man to clarify his story to them over a cup of hot coffee with milk. He sat at the table, uncertain how he should act or why he was there, and in between sentences he let his eyes span the dining room, noticing pictures of the young girl; pictures of her with a man and a woman who were much younger than the couple who now sat across from him. Over coffee, he relayed the story. He told them of where he found her and of the rain and why he picked her up and he told them how he dropped her off. He even described the clothing she wore and the contradiction between her gratuitous smile and the sad look in her eyes. When he was finished, he sipped his coffee and he waited for the man and woman to respond.

The man and the woman appeared sad and yet practiced at telling their story. They first began by apologizing for his inconvenience. Before the truck driver had a chance to ask why they were sorry, they explained.

It seems she had passed many years ago and many travelers over the years had stopped, as he did that night, detailing the same story of the lovely young lady who asked for a ride in the rain—the appreciative smile, the sad eyes, the supposed car trouble. They told of the day when she was trying to get home and they explained the details of the crash. The truth was she died on a similar rainy night when her car slid over the cliff—*la curva de muerte*. Being so high up into the mountain, the roads did not have proper lighting and she, being in such a hurry to see her mother and father, lost control of the car and died. Now her story has become a song, a lesson for those who don't pay attention while driving through the mountain. But she has not been the only one. Many had suffered the same fate and still many had died after her.

The young man got chills up his spine and he shivered a moment in the passenger seat when the fisherman was finished telling him the story.

"That, they say, is what the truck driver did when her parents told him the story," Don Fidel said.

The young man turned to face the driver, and then he turned to face the world as it passed him by on the road. "That is such a terrible story. So sad. I couldn't imagine trying to write that story."

"Here," Don Fidel said, handing the young man a cigarette. "It will help you relax."

"*Gracias.*"

Don Fidel wrestled with the steering wheel and balanced himself enough to light his own cigarette. He breathed in heavy and blew the smoke out like he was blowing out candles on a birthday cake. "*De veras.* It is a sad story. But the world is full of them, stories of tragedy and loss, but there are stories of happiness, too, although they don't seem to come from Mexico."

"Is that why Mexicans drink so much when they listen to them?"

Don Fidel laughed so hard he nearly drove the truck onto a nearby curb and, despite regaining control of the steering wheel, he continued to laugh. "You always make me smile, *niño!*"

The young man was trying to be comical and it worked. Hearing the story relayed the way Don Fidel told it made him very sad. It also made him wonder if he could ever write a happy story, because most of his works were sad, too. "It had to be terrible to be the girl's parents, because not only did they lose a child, but a song was written and now many people know about it."

"I never thought of it that way, but perhaps you are right. Except most of the *corridos* that we sing are written years later, after a story becomes settled," he said, using a free hand to make a pounding motion into his chest. "They are settled in the hearts of men. They are translated into songs after they have been transformed into a part of our souls. To write them and sing them the way we do may seem like disrespect to you because you are not from here. But, in fact, they honor those who have died."

"I don't know if I want anyone singing songs about my death when I am gone," the young man said.

The two of them arrived at a small boat ramp near a large bridge, and Don Fidel found a place to park under a large palm tree. He set the shifter in the park position and, before addressing the boy, he took one last drag of his cigarette, and then tossed it onto the ground outside.

"You are a special boy. You have a gift of touching people's lives with your stories. And someday people all over the world may know your name and they may honor you with writings of your deeds when you pass, but you must realize that not all of us will be treated that way when we die." Don Fidel became still and stared out into the water in front of them, allowing the boy to watch his eyes follow the interior and exterior of his pickup truck—the rust stains on the hood, the chips and cracks in the front windshield, the weathered dashboard, the loose and frayed wires where a radio was once mounted.

Then, he said to him, "I will die a poor man. I once had a wife and children, you know this, and they are gone now. My wife has died and my children have moved on, some of them to do better with their lives and others because they were better than me. I have my father's house and this truck and enough money to feed myself and when I am really hungry I catch my own dinner in the ocean. I have you and I call you friend, but I am poor and I will die a poor man."

The young man felt sad for his friend and tried to interrupt him. "Hey that's not true, you have lots of friends."

"No," Don Fidel said with a wave of his hand. "You are my friend, but you are a young man and I am old and you have lots of life yet to live and I have very little. And I have learned that life is short and precious, and to waste a gift that God has given you is the same as to waste an entire life. I once heard the whispers as you do. I once felt the stirring in my soul, but I ignored it. I chose not to listen and now I sit on my porch with my beers at night and I listen to the *corridos* on the radio and I wonder where my life could have ended, and how much my children might have loved me, and how much more I could have offered my wife. She had dreams and her dreams were to see me fulfill mine. But I did not. I wasted my gifts by ignoring the whispers of my own soul."

Don Fidel reached for the boy's hand and said, "I am proud of you. You have done well with your life and it has been my pleasure having you to share your stories with me."

"We'll be friends as long..." the young man started, wishing he could take back the sentence he started. "We'll be friends as long as we can."

"Maybe someday someone will write the song of my life?" Don Fidel said. He turned away from the boy, unable to look him in the eyes, and he fought back a pain in his heart and he repeated himself two or three more times as if he were convincing himself that his life could somehow become a benefit to others. *Maybe someday someone will write the song of my life.*

His wife had a habit of telling him in Spanish, do not die a wicked and slothful person. She often paraphrased scripture and, in this regard, she was reminding him of the story of the master who gave gifts and talents to three of his servants, each one receiving less than the other and the third only receiving one. The master gave to each of the three servants according to their own abilities and departed. When the master returned, he learned that the first and second servants each doubled their talents, or gifts, but the third servant did not. This third servant, for fear of failing, hid his talent in the Earth and because of this, he was removed of all his gifts. They were given to the first two servants.

In considering his life on this day, Don Fidel was ashamed of himself and fearful. His heart was heavy with sadness and he missed his wife and his children. The older he became, the more he missed his wife and often, when he was alone, he found that he could not remember the sounds his children made when they were playing. He might have forgotten their faces were it not for the many pictures he had mounted on the walls of his home. He had lived a tough life. Pain and loss had become as familiar to him as the acquaintance of the young man. He understood thirst and hunger and solitude and he carried with him the fear that no one would be there to aid him in his most dire moment of necessity. He would carry this fear with him until his death.

"I think your life would make a wonderful story, Don Fidel."

Don Fidel Cristiano smiled and slapped the young man on the hand. "*Andale!* Let's go fishing, *mi amigo!*"

He looked at the young man and he thought, *You are lucky—yet not so lucky.* In all his years of appreciating the tales of Mexico and all the nights he ignored the whispers in his sleep, Don Fidel knew that greater pains awaited those who chose to tell the stories of the world, because he knew the price of such experiences. He knew the boy would write about love only after his heart had been broken, and he would write about loss after suffering to live without those he cared for. He was aware that the boy would taste hunger and thirst and sacrifice and he would wear many hats to obtain the essence of the experiences that life had to offer before he could write of them. The fisherman could not bring himself to tell his friend this. He would leave that lesson to fate's hand.

The young man sat still for a moment, allowing his friend to remove himself from the truck and he watched him as he gathered together their fishing reels and tackle, and he watched him as he set himself down upon a stump along the boat ramp. The old man set his bait upon his hooks and tossed his lines as far as he could cast them into the water, and he lit a cigarette and shielded the sun from his eyes, looking back towards the truck. With a smile, he waved the boy over.

"I'm coming, my friend," the young man said under his breath. "There are stories waiting to be caught in the ocean today."

The two men fished that entire day, and they talked and they laughed and the fisherman made fun of the boy for his lack of experiences, and the boy helped his friend in every way he could. He figured he owed him that much. He figured *life* owed him that much. He didn't think it was fair to pay such a heavy price for ignoring fate's call to claim his gift of writing. The young man listened to his friend tell of other *corridos*, other stories of loss and of suffering and of death, and they sat at the boat ramp that entire night.

Don Fidel Cristiano was a fisherman and he sat on the boat ramp with his only friend, a young man many years his junior and he sang his *corridos*.

They caught only one fish that night and it seemed to matter little to either of them.

About the author:

My name is Bobby Ozuna and I was born and raised in Ft. Worth, Texas. I have been working to develop my writing skills for over six years. I completed my first literary novel, *Proud Souls*, in the fall of 2005 and I have since been seeking literary representation for this piece. As many newcomers to this business may find, it is often easier to put the words on paper than it is to get someone credible to read them, but still I press on. I am in the re-write stages of my second novel, *The Righteous* and somehow I have managed to produce four new chapters to a story I will call, "The Other Side of Glory." I am the author of several short stories, one of which received recognition in the Tarrant County College Spring writing contest in early 2003 and another placed as a top-twenty finalist of over 420 submission in the Gather.com short-story competition last year. I am honored to present to you my latest work and my first published story which I have entitled "Corrido." I have been working within the Information Technology market for seven years and I am currently employed by a Managed Service Provider in the Fort Worth area. I am the fourth child in a family of five and I am the father of four beautiful children—Elizabeth, Lazaro, Dominic and Damian—and late at night, when all the world is asleep and I am plagued by the desires of my inner muse, I am a writer. You can keep up with my writing here: inotauthor.gather.com

BEAUTIFUL MEN
©2007 by Vanessa Orlando

A tremor vibrated through Cassie's nervous system, the veins and arteries of her body carrying a charge that shook her a few centimeters to the left and right. She put her empty wine glass on the table, threw the reunion newsletter next to it and stared at the name.

Steven Porter. Class dreamboat, blonde and blue-eyed—back when blonde and blue-eyed was something a person wanted to be.

Cassie smirked. So many stupid girls wasted perfectly good afternoons scribbling his name on book covers, circling it with hearts and flowers until the ink ran out. What they all wouldn't have done to be her, the cool girl at the Senior Party with the illicit vodka she'd gulped down in large shots; the girl beautiful Steven Porter picked to anoint in the back seat of his car before heading off to the "big leagues."

Cassie filled a lemonade glass with wine and ice and held it up to the window to watch the sun beam through it. She had to admit, *that* memory had legs.

> *Beautiful men like Steven Porter—even before they are full-grown men—demand all consuming, out-of-control passion more than laughter, more than truth, more than love. A controlled life, a restrained adventure, a checked obsession makes life bland, even sour. Cassie will nurture his passion -- plant it, water it, make it grow. She will never trim it or tie it or cover it in burlap. She will feed the creature so that her own life will become spectacular.*

Cassie finished her wine, picked up the registration form and glanced back at the newsletter:

ORANGE GROVE HIGH SCHOOL'S TWENTY-FIVE YEAR REUNION - CONFIRMED ATTENDEES: MR. AND MRS. STEVEN PORTER

Cassie clicked a pen on and off, slowly, rhythmically, as if to gently pump up her courage, but her thumb picked up the pace until the non-stop *tic-tak-tic-tak-tic-tak* instilled in her a sense of urgency, telling her over and over that too much time had passed, and if she didn't send that form in now, *right now*, she would never see Steven Porter again. Not everyone got a second chance, but here was hers—theirs, hand delivered by U.S. Post.

Cassie chewed on the clip of the pen, shaving off the plastic with her teeth. She really did graduate from the University of Central Florida with a psychology degree, as she wrote on her registration form, but she had never headed up a research team that presented a paper on the manifestation of Alzheimer's disease in fraternal twins at the University of Bonn. (Who would check?) Her favorite high school music was—ah—Mozart and Led Zeppelin. Her favorite hobby was, let's see, sky diving? No. Mountain climbing? No, no. Antique collecting. Her favorite high school memory? She clicked the pen even faster. Steven Porter's backseat.

Cassie folded the form carefully into the envelope and licked the flap, the wine and glue blending together in a bitter paste. She traced the edges of the envelope, and then looked at the pads of her fingers as if she'd expected the envelope to draw blood.

Beautiful men have so many choices—an always available assembly line of big bosoms and pouty lips to choose from, and there are never any repercussions for moving on too quickly as long as they come back. Even if they come back twenty-five years later. Cassie has no smorgasbord of all-you-can-eat lovers. She doesn't need them. Not now. Not if Steven Porter's coming home.

Cassie filled her glass again. What did twenty-five years do to beautiful, perfect Steven Porter? Maybe he'd gotten thick around the middle and bald up top. Maybe he married a shrew of a woman who bore idiot children who cared nothing about his glory days. Maybe he'd lost a bundle in the stock market, suffered from high blood pressure, become an insurance salesman. Maybe life had finally taken him down a goddamn notch.

Or maybe...maybe beautiful Steven Porter was finally ready to come back where he belonged. All kinds of people told their families they were going to run out to buy cigarettes or bread and never returned home. Instead, they started new lives, with new partners, in more exotic places. If Cassie did everything right, Steven Porter might finally start planning his own trip to the corner store.

Beautiful men smile and in that tone of voice only beautiful men have (you know, that low growl that makes you laugh and roll your eyes when ordinary men try it), he will call you "baby" like it's your name. The earnestness in his voice will implore you to understand how much you will always mean to him. Always. Soon, though, you will catch a perfume scent you don't recognize as you realize he hasn't called you "baby" since you can remember. He is gone before he leaves, and you will immediately turn up the volume in your head so you can't hear it. Oh baby, don't be that way; you know it didn't mean anything. *Now, though, it's different. Now it will be Cassie's perfume another woman smells. Cassie's perfume all over perfect Steven Porter.*

***

Cassie squealed when she saw Ashley, and squealed again when she saw Sharon, and then held up her wine glass and yelled "oh my god!" loud enough for the kitchen staff to hear when she saw Pricilla.

"The four musketeers," she yelled. "Reunited at last."

Cassie had seen them only once after graduation: around Christmas time, in a mall coffee shop where they were eating lunch. They didn't come home much, they'd said, because it took too much time and money to fly home from New York...Chicago...Seattle, places like that.

"I can't believe it's been twenty-five years," said Ashley, squeezing Sharon. "Where did the time go?"

Each woman wiped her eyes while trying to keep her mascara in place. On some hidden cue, it seemed, they began a rapid-fire exchange of memories that they hadn't thought about in years.

Yes, who could forget those drive-in movies and piling everyone into Bobby Jenson's car on Dollar-A-Car Night? Cassie laughed loud to prove she enjoyed the memory.

Yes, they remembered the senior class play where Roberta Summerland kept forgetting her lines. Cassie did a spit take with her wine to prove she recalled it.

Yes, they remembered that lovely girl elected Homecoming Queen but, ohmagosh no, Cassie hadn't heard she'd committed suicide eight years ago. What a terrible tragedy. What was her name again?

A bell seemed to go off, indicating the lightning round had ended and it was time to fast forward twenty-five years to where they were now.

"Two marriages and three kids for me," said Pricilla.

"One marriage for me, but it'll be over officially next month," Ashley said wryly.

"Fifteen years for me," said Cassie, raising her wine glass. "Five years the first time, three years the second time, four years the third time, and three years the last time."

The women went silent and looked at one another before looking back to Cassie.

"Kids?" asked Sharon.

"God, no. What about you?"

"Oh, wait, let me guess," said Ashley, locking arms with her old friend. "Sharon's been married to the same perfect man for twenty years. They still have sex four times a week and have two perfectly perfect children. Am I close?"

"Pretty close," she said laughing.

"God, Shar, you are *so* boring."

The four middle-aged women cackled like flighty teenagers and went on to the next lightning round, each one turning about but keeping the others nearby.

"Alice, yes, of course I remember you."

"Gary, yes, of course I remember you."

"Linda, my god, how *are* you?"

Cassie stepped to the bar and looked around the room, first quickly, then slowly, studying each face in case Steven Porter had somehow managed to age badly. She sighed impatiently. Where the hell was he? As the bartender poured the wine, Cassie tapped the glass until he filled it completely.

> *Ordinary woman sometimes grow into great beauties. Stunning beauties. Unfathomable, magnificent beauties. But overweight Pricilla didn't. And overdone Ashley couldn't possibly. And unfashionable Sharon tried, but self-respecting middle-aged women do not wear pink Capri pants. Cassie Warrington, though, has kept her body tight and toned, her skin clear and smooth. She has a squadron of hairdressers and make-up experts, an army of personal trainers and yoga gurus. There is no sin in being ordinary. Or rather, no sin in other people being ordinary, but Cassie—she wants no part of ordinary.*

Cassie heard a murmur rumble slowly through the room. Intermittently, she heard voices say, "Porter,"

"…baseball…"

"…such a crush…"

"…Steven…"

Cassie froze, as if a slight movement would make him disappear the way even a tiny sound makes a bird fly away. When she turns around, she thought, the place will go dark, pitch black. She envisions spotlights hitting them as they see each other for the first time in…is it really twenty-five years? She imagines him walking toward her with determination, ignoring everyone else. Both of them, of course, will open their arms and, with quivering chins, say, "I've missed you." Everyone will applaud, some will weep, and Steve Porter will press his body to hers and never stop.

Cassie squeezed the bartender's arm. *Pay attention*, she wanted to say, *you are about to see a love story*. The bartender shook her hand off without looking up. She was going to turn around now. Turn around and see Steven Porter right behind her.

> *Ah, if only Beautiful Men came with warning labels. Warning: The Surgeon General has determined that beautiful men will*

make you believe you are the center of the universe and then single-handedly, and very quickly, destroy that universe. Beware. Tread Carefully. Avoid Close Contact.

Cassie took quick sips of her wine as she watched Steven Porter shake hands with a man she didn't recognize. She sipped again as another man clasped his shoulder and shook hands, and then another, and another, until he stood in a circle, smiling with seven or eight, then nine people.

Damn, he was handsome. Six-feet-two and tanned naturally by the sun, not a tanning booth. Still fit and muscular. And blonde? Steven Porter's neon blonde hair reflected the rays from the overhead light and made him glow like gold, his aura visible to anyone who looked.

Cassie watched him focus those blue eyes on whoever he was talking to, and then watched that person move closer to him. Each time, he threw his head back in laughter. Even in silhouette, he was charming.

Nature did not invent beautiful men so they could be treated as if they were common. Beautiful men, like wild zoo animals, must be displayed but contained, revered but controlled, free but shackled all at once. Their enormous power, their terrifying strength, their unmatched splendor must be rendered impotent before they can be appreciated and protected. Steven Porter, like lions, like bears, must be caught and caged. And Cassie, if she does everything right, will own the only key.

Cassie sipped quickly on her wine and examined the woman he clutched to his side. She was young, too young, *ridiculously* young. She had a body like plywood, thin and flat with small bumps here and there for breasts, hips, and knees; not a curve or soft spot anywhere. Steven Porter kept his arm around her as they worked the room like veteran politicians, both of them knowing how short or long their steps should be, as if they'd done this sort of thing a thousand times before.

"I figured he'd marry a Plain Jane type," said Pricilla.

"Maybe she's rich," said Cassie.

"Or great in bed," said Ashley, the three of them bursting into giggles.

Cassie clutched her stomach. Why weren't his eyes scanning the room? Didn't he read the final list of RSVPs? Didn't he peruse the sign-in sheets like she had?

"Do you think he'll remember us?" asked Pricilla.

"Us? Probably not, but I bet he'll remember Sharon," Ashley said.

At that moment, Steven Porter looked up, pointed at Sharon as if he knew exactly where she'd be, and, with a brilliant smile, blew her an exaggerated kiss. Cassie leaned toward Sharon to prevent it from landing, to redirect its path to the proper receiver. Steven Porter seemed to purse his lips a little, but when he turned away, Cassie realized he hadn't seen her.

"God, he's still yummy, isn't he, Shar?" said Ashley, exaggerating a sigh. "I wonder what he's doing now."

Sharon smiled. "He's a youth counselor; been running a teen center outside Seattle for about eight years now. He loves it, too. He's never been happier."

The women stopped as if they'd been reading a script and the next page was missing.

"And that so called Plain Jane?" said Sharon, "That's not his wife, that's his daughter Chloe. She's studying to be a veterinarian."

Cassie finished her wine in one swallow and stepped backwards. "How the hell do you know that?"

Ashley stood in front of Sharon, and then moved in closer until their foreheads met, just like they used to do twenty-five years ago when one of them had a secret.

Sharon winked.

"You little slut," Ashley laughed, throwing an arm around her old friend.

"What? What?" asked Pricilla and Cassie at the same time.

"Hell, I'd still be married, too, if I was getting a piece of *that* every night," Ashley said pointing at Steven Porter.

"What are you *talking* about?" Cassie hissed, a small spray of spit hitting Sharon's hand.

"Chloe's his daughter," said Sharon, pointing. "And *my* daughter."

Except for Cassie, the women howled together, repeating, "Oh my god" and "you're kidding" over and over, each trying to say something, but stopping after a word or phrase to laugh and say "oh my god" again.

"Why didn't you tell us?" said Pricilla.

"Well, it's not news to me. I'd forgotten what a big fan club he had in all of you."

"Wait a minute, wait a minute," Cassie said, her voice going up, and then sliding back to almost a whisper. "You married Steven Porter? You married him?"

"Nineteen years now."

"Nineteen years?" Cassie whispered.

"Remember how he went to play pro baseball after high school? Well, he broke his leg about a year later and then spent a few more years trying to get back into the pros, but he just couldn't run like he used to. He got pretty depressed about it. Well," said Sharon laughing, "one day, he just showed up on my doorstep and he never left."

"Oh, good for you," said Ashley. "But hey, I always thought you two were made for each other. Didn't I always tell you that?"

Cassie felt her face flush. *He never left?*

Cassie took Pricilla's full wine glass, replacing it with her empty, and walked toward the rest room, focusing on the stick figure of a woman by the door. She heard someone say, "Cassie? Cassie Warrington, is that you?" but she stayed focused on the stick figure, as if she was tight rope walking and one misstep would send her plummeting into a black hole forever.

Beautiful men must marry not just beautiful women, but elegant women. Women with precise, head-turning features and flawlessly blended skin tones. Their cheeks have to be higher, their eyes greener, their muscle structures inherently, biologically superior from what you find around here. It is a law. Of nature. Of common sense. Beautiful men like Steven Porter do not marry women who look like pudgy, overdone Sharon; do not carry the seeds of ugly, nasty looking children. They can't. They mustn't.

Cassie held a wet towel over her eyes, her mascara turning into long black streaks. Clearly, her old friends were joking. Surely they remembered how painfully in love she and Steven Porter were, how losing her virginity to him was such a coup, only to have it fall into agony when he left for spring training the next day. All three of them, certainly, were just trying to see how long she'd stay silent before calling their bluff. They were probably plotting more Candid Camera scenes to laugh about now.

Sharon married to Steven Porter? How absurd! How insane! Her friends had played with her like this before. Twenty-five years ago, Pricilla and Ashley said they saw her go into the back of Steven Porter's car, and then told everyone Cassie was too drunk to notice it wasn't Steven Porter she was with, but his creepy buddy Steve Wilson.

Let them play, Cassie thought as she pressed the towel harder.

"Are you okay?"

It was a voice she didn't recognize.

"Fine," she muttered quietly. "Just fine."

When she took the towel from her eyes, Cassie could not comprehend what she saw. Chloe was not stunning from a distance, and now, up close, she wasn't even attractive. Her dull beige skin had noticeable dry patches. Her brown hair was mousey and straight and full of split ends. Her hands were badly in need of a manicure. Beautiful, perfect Steven Porter could not possibly be responsible for such a thing.

"Do you want to sit down? There's a couch over there," Chloe said.

Cassie began to see orange circles closing in, but breathed in deeply enough to hold them back. *Do this right,* Cassie thought. *Do this right.* So, she let Chloe guide her to the couch.

"Did you go to school here?" Cassie asked. "I mean…obviously, this isn't your reunion, but did you go to Orange Grove High?"

"Oh no," laughed Chloe, "I've never even lived in Florida. My mom and dad went here. Steve and Sharon Porter. Do you know them?"

Steve and Sharon Porter. Cassie pressed the towel to her face again. "I know them," she said, looking up. "I just talked to your mother. She calls you Plain Jane. But in a nice way."

Chloe reared back, the smile shaking to stay on her face as she looked at herself in the mirror and ran her fingers through her hair.

"Did I bring my glass in here?"

Chloe picked up the empty wine glass. "This it?"

"Yes, please," said Cassie, extending her arm.

"It's empty."

"That's okay."

"My mom and dad came into town yesterday," Chloe said. "I had finals so I couldn't come until today. My dad just picked me up from the airport and was supposed to drop me off at my grandmother's, but he talked me into coming with him."

"Snake oil," Cassie hissed.

"What?"

She sighed loudly. "Your father is a very charming man, a very handsome man. Do you know that?"

"Yeah, I know," Chloe said, smiling. "*All* my friends get crushes on him."

"And he's probably very nice to them, isn't he?"

"Of course."

"Your dear, precious father can make anyone believe anything. I'll prove it to you."

Cassie curled her index finger back and forth, motioning for the girl to come closer. Chloe hesitated but took the step.

"Look in the mirror. Do you see?"

"See what?"

"Do you see any of your father in you?"

"My hair is the same…"

"Oh god. Snake oil! Snake oil! Wake up."

"But…"

"It's so obvious. Are you stupid? Your father isn't your father. If he was, you wouldn't be such an ugly thing. Look!"

Chloe gasped.

"The milkman," Cassie laughed. "Sharon obviously fucked the milkman."

Cassie walked across the restroom and used all her strength to thrust open the door. For god sakes, he'd left her in the backseat of that car. Not so much as a thank you. Just left her there because he was done. She was still in the backseat the next morning, half naked and covered with vomit; and perfect, beautiful Steven Porter acted surprised, like he had no idea what she was doing there. Just kept muttering, "*Asshole! I'm sick of his crap!*"

Steven Porter then called his parents, and they called hers, and her father pulled her out of the car by the hair and slapped her right in front of them until she apologized. *She* apologized! Beautiful men were always getting away with hit-or-miss love affairs. Give it a try in the backseat, son, and walk away if you don't like it, and don't worry about the consequences.

Cassie is a stupid woman. A classic dumb bitch. What on earth would a beautiful man like Steven Porter get from a gentle touch or rough tumble with her that he hasn't gotten from a thousand other women he doesn't even remember? Beautiful men create dead-end desires and touchless sensations that Cassie can only imagine. But dear god, she does imagine them. Over and over, they haunt her. Torment her. She can't shake them or hide from them. How could she ever believe a man like beautiful, terrible Steven Porter would crave her, yearn for her? Cassie is a stupid, stupid woman.

The restroom door swung open fast as Cassie shoved, but it stopped abruptly without hitting the wall.

"*Ahhkk*," she heard a man yelp. Then other voices.

"Oh my."

"Oh gosh."

"What in the world?"

"You okay, Steve?"

Cassie caught the door as it rushed back toward her, then peered around it and laughed. There he was. Up close. Tall, blonde, perfect Steven Porter. He rubbed his elbow lightly, more for show than to relieve any pain, and looked at Cassie as if he expected her to say something.

With black streaks still running out of her eyes, Cassie walked toward Steven Porter. She tripped on her shoe that had somehow come lose from her foot. Her empty wine glass shook in her hands as she reached toward him.

"Cigarettes, Steven?" she winked. "Bread?"

Steven Porter smiled uneasily and cocked his head. Chloe rushed out of the restroom and stood between them to shield her father from incoming shrapnel. Steven Porter's eyes narrowed as his little girl whispered in his perfectly golden ear. He put his arms around her and stared menacingly at Cassie, as if she were poison, as if she'd spent all night in his car and he didn't know why, as if he'd never touched her in his life.

Cassie lunged for his arm, to guide him out of this place, but she missed, lost her balance, tripped and stumbled to the floor. If Steven Porter or anyone else offered to help her up, she didn't notice.

Beautiful men are mystics, turning love into hate with the tap of a cane, the snap of a finger, the wink of an eye. Years of make-believe enchantment turn into searing regret when the illusion is exposed, the punch line revealed. Cassie's perfect love, perfect joy, perfect life—it all belongs to Sharon. Sharon Porter. Not a beautiful woman or even an attractive woman, but a chosen one. An anointed one. Cassie is on the floor, inconsolable in the face of the irreconcilable. She will be there a very long time.

About the author:

Vanessa Orlando is a two-time recipient of the Maryland Writers Association Short Fiction Prize and a Georgia Associated Press Feature writing award. Her short story "When Sara Looks Up" was made into a short film by Columbia College Chicago in 2004. Her latest piece, "Railroading the Devil," appears in *Enhanced Gravity: More Fiction by Washington Area Women*, published in June 2006 by Paycock Press (and available through amazon.com and D.C. area bookstores). She was also one of five writers selected for the Manitoba Writer's Guild's Emerging Writers Program in 2000. Vanessa has two dogs and two cats—all rescues—and is an active volunteer with YorkieRescueMe.com, a nonprofit organization dedicated to saving Yorkshire Terriers and Yorkie mixes.

LESSONS FROM THE GYPSY CAMP
©2004 By Elizabeth Appell
ISBN: 0-9742652-1-7

Available on the Scribes Valley Publishing Website:
www.scribesvalley.com

Or

Any number of online bookstores

Scribes Valley Publishing
Knoxville, TN